AUTHOR'S NOTE

While Alcoholics Anonymous is discussed in this story,
it is not an endorsement of the program.
Our tenet is "attraction rather than promotion."
We are here if you need us.

This book is dedicated to Andrew, Samuel, and Jack.
You know my story, for you lived it too.
Go with your instincts, for this story could be yours as well.
How do you know I love you?
"Because you tell us every day."

PROLOGUE

"I thought you'd think it was responsible for me to call."

"I'd think it was responsible of you not to drink in the first place. You're seventeen, Jason, for Christ's sake. Think, son."

"I did think. I called you, just like you always said. 'Son,' you said. 'If you are out drinking, call if you need a ride. Always call.'"

"It's 2:30, Jason."

"Sorry. I didn't know 'Dad's taxi' had operating hours."

"Tone, son. Watch the tone. When we drink we sometimes get irrational."

"Christ."

"Jason, enough."

Exactly. I stared out the window, slouched uncomfortably in the silent static of AM news radio and the coldness of soggy tee, damp from beer bong spillage and upside-down keg-stand runoff.

"So, how was the party?" Dad asked. An afterthought. I think he was talking to me.

His program now over, he clicked off the dial and with a sigh, he shook his head and went on about *that president of ours*.

And still I stared, breathing hard off the window to see if my night smelled as bad as it tasted, wondering how the other boys had gotten home and suddenly remembering the deal with Cruz.

CHAPTER ONE
FRIDAY

1. Jason, Brian, and the Ride

Word was the guy's name was Brent, that he attended a local prep school, and that he had been accepted to Cornell, only because his father was a platinum contributor to the alumni association; for Brent was, according to my best friend Brian, a "slacker pothead."

Word also was that the guy's parents were "summering" for a week on some Cape Cod island---Nantucket or Martha's Vineyard, whatever---and their high school graduation gift to him was the option *not* to go.

A little taste of independence before University, eh, boy? A noogie to the head, a playful tousle of his Abercrombie hair.

Rightee-O, pops. A punch to the arm. *Rightee-O.*

By the standards of *my* crowd---accustomed, as we were, to gatherings at the abandoned airstrip, or at developing cul-de-sacs illuminated by strategically-angled headlights---a house party was a house party, wherever it was held. However, a year-end bash at the Country Club was very, very attractive, and excited chatter began weeks in advance.

There really were only three in that "crowd" of mine. First, there was my best friend Brian, a rising second-year at the community college but whom I had met during his senior year at Premier. Brian had overheard two hottie check-out chibs at the mall's J. Crew gabbing on about the Brent gig, and because I had already told him about the party he had his introductory conversation piece, which found him leaving the mall with a sharp new outfit and two phone numbers.

Then there were Jed and Chat, my other "close" friends, who had opted out of higher education in pursuit of upward mobility through telemarketing for a home improvement franchise. Jed and Chat were regulars at the mall's food court and adjacent arcade. It was their daily outlet from the tedium of telephone sales-pitch and inevitable hang-ups. It was also the contact and social information mecca of the tri-county area, so they were privy to the party long before either Brian or me.

It was at the food court that Jed and Chat met Slang (not a friend at all), who sold fake ID's, among other black market commodities, from burned bootlegged concerts to authentic Grateful Dead smoking paraphernalia, and for $150 a piece we were all of legal drinking age as declared by the Great State of Wyoming, unanimously chosen not only because of its distance from everything, but also for its awesomely cool Latin motto, cedant arma togae, or "yield to the toga."

Although neither Jed nor Chat appeared destined for great things, they were resourceful, and they did have their people. And Brian had the ride, an aged Ford Taurus but a ride nonetheless, as well as a few connections to college frat life.

And I, a rising senior at the city's honor school, aptly named City Premier, was the perfect counter to this mediocrity and deficiency, the Brains of the outfit: from future Yalie to Peace Corps volunteer, master's to PhD, laureate to emeritus.

Father could see it now.

But first, I had some work to do, beginning with the intensive summer SAT prep courses in critical reading and mathematics that most assuredly would help better my initial 1780 fiasco earlier that spring---*Jason, what on earth were you thinking?*---by at least 200 points, as the program boasted; then, to boost my GPA while it still mattered, and to pick up some extracurricular interests that did not involve my base friends---they being Brian, Jed, and Chat--- whose names Father either mispronounced, or forgot altogether, but to whom as a group he *always* referred as Huey, Dewey, and Louie.

I had sociology last period of the day, and as there were only three days of classes left, and this was Friday, I bailed early, again, accepting with bitter remorse that there was no way to improve my 38 average. Not now, not at this late date.

Brian met me outside the cafeteria of the school, his alma mater, the Taurus rumbling softly, wheezing asthmatically.

"I've decided to name her 'Rocinante'," Brian satisfactorily declared when I entered, as if having pondered the issue at great lengths. He handed me a beer. "Whatcha think?"

"Her?"

"The car, dumbass. It is a Taurus, after all, and she and I have traveled many great, mysterious roads together, just as that Quixote dude did with his horse. I saw it this morning on A&E. Now, seatbelt, dude. She's been bucking a bit lately. Been a bit orn'ry."

Brian always wore his seatbelt, and insisted that others do the same. I clicked mine, and drank deeply as we pulled away.

"Bri, I'm pretty certain I've failed soash." I looked at him, though by his glaze and petrified smirk it was obvious his thoughts were still on his car. "I mean," I continued, "there's really no extra credit to be done with a 38, especially not with three days 'til exams."

"Dude, listen," Brian said, snapping out of his reverie. "A, sociology's an elective; and B, you have the test. Ace that, and you're fine. Markowski'll probably even boost you up a couple points, thinking *he* made a mistake in his calculations somewhere. Everyone loves a success story." Brian placed his empty in the cardboard twelve between his ankles, groped around for two more, and handed them to me. "And C, finish your damn beer. You got some catching up to do."

"Are you sure he gives the same exam every year? I mean, positive? We're talking serious shit here, Bri. I can't be failing anything." I handed him his opened beer and he propped it between his legs.

"D, E, and F, abso-fucking-lutely, and I have your copy. We've discussed this. Now shut up about school and let's discuss Ro-ci-NAN-te." He rolled the R. "So, whatcha think? The name?" His eyes and smile were wide and he nodded his head spasmodically.

"Brian," I sighed, impatiently shaking my head. "Taurus is a fucking bull. If the piece of shit deserves a name, call it Babe." I wiped beer foam from my mouth with my sleeve. "Or shit. There ya go. Call it 'shit,' as in 'Bull-shit,' which is exactly what it is and exactly what you're full of."

I slammed my second beer, washing down the week and the reality of failure; and, adding the two empties to the MacDonald's-large-fry-container-and-junk-mail clutter at my feet, I shifted uncomfortably in the silence.

Rocinante my ass. Damn car didn't even have a radio.

How did I get so deep in this thing? What happened? Too many damn Fridays, leaving school early. Always an excuse. Even IF Brian has the test, which he'd better, there are still so many variables. You don't just fail an elective. It doesn't happen. That's supposed to be the gimme grade, like gym.

A 38. Damn. Bill's gonna shit.

"Jay?" Brian asked sheepishly after three stop lights, handing me the rest of his beer as a peace offering.

"What."

"Sorry, man. Really. I know your old man Bill's been riding you pretty hard. Let's just try to have fun tonight, okay? How's about it?"

"Sure, dude. Sorry too." I slapped and shook his knee and dismissed the future, finished his beer and grabbed the case of empties from between his ankles and pointed to a convenient mart.

"Oh, and Jay?"

"Don't worry, I got some cash for the next round."

"No, that's not it, but that's cool too."

"What then?"

"Babe won't work either, man. Dude's an ox."

2. Moderation is the Key

Brian worked what he called "three quarters time" as an assistant manager at the Silver Bullet Luxury Carwash Service to pay for his apartment and his college tuition, which was an absolutely perfect job for one vain enough to think a fully detailed ride heightened score potential with the ladies.

So, the afternoon was spent sunning ourselves on the benches outside the Bullet, drinking the second twelve from forty-ounce strawed thermoses while Roz got her extreme body make over for an evening with Country Club high society.

"Bri, no matter how you dress her up, she's always gonna be a '92 Ford Taurus." The absolutely best way to rid my mind of academia was to toss around weighty topics after several beers with Brian. He was good for that. "Breed her with a Porsche, a 911 Carrera, and the best case scenario result might be a Honda Civic. Best case, Bri."

"Jayman, I'm shocked. I truly am. Roz could meet a, a Pinto, you know, one of her own kind---I'd like to keep it in the family---and through gross complications she could bear an El Camino. An *El Camino*, Jay. And you know what? *You know what?* I'd buy that little baby spic mobile some dice and spinners and I'd drive him myself, proudly, flashing my pearly white grill, waving at all the pretty chiblets as if he were my very own, Jay. Sometimes you really worry me. Fine father you'll make."

"Him?"

"Carl, sand the floor, man. Sand the floor. Like this," he called in his best Anglo-Japanese, making quick circular patterns in the air with his palms facing the boy, who was working feverishly on the car's lustre.

Brian loved his extended cable, and often made obscure references to old television and movie reruns.

"Wax on, wax off. On, off. That's better, Carl San." He slowly, silently pantomimed the routine a few more times. "Sorry, Jay. Sometimes I gotta bust out the Mr. Miyagi *Karate Kid* action on the new boys. Anyhow, what now?"

"Him. Why is the El Camino a 'him,' and your precious Taurus a 'she' as if it were a fucking ship on its maiden voyage?"

"'El,' my friend, is masculine, as is 'camin-O,' Spanish for 'the road.' Comprende' amig-O?"

"Amazing. You know your Spanish, but you thought Taurus was a horse. You're a fucking miracle."

"Jason, the zodiac is for the weak that need direction. Now, gimme."

Brian sucked up the remaining piss-warm foam from his thermos while motioning me to do the same. "Moderation. Moderation is the key, Bri. You taught me that. Long night ahead of us."

"Jason Ottomar Braswell," Brian continued, imitating my father's instructive voice, "the beer will get warm, and you know how irresponsible it is to waste what has been graciously bestowed unto us via the one they call Slang and the Great State of Wyoming. That is not sound Ivy thinking, son. Cogito, my boy."

Brian went to give his finished car a once over---from my standpoint, a hard rain would have done the same job---and I went to his broom-closet office to pour into our sippees the remaining six beers and to discard the evidence in the Arby's dumpster next door.

I had drunk eight beers in three hours; finishing the sippee would make it eleven, and drinking through a straw pronounced the effect. I hadn't anything to eat in five hours, and that was three Premier fried beef nuggets, boiled summer squash and a fruit cup. I needed something solid in my stomach if I wanted to stay glued.

3. The Pull

I tossed the bag of sandwiches into Brian's lap and put both sippees into the large cup holders Brian had the foresight to buy specially from Wal-Mart to accommodate sippees.

"Smells nice. Shiny too. Nice, shiny plastic."

Brian pulled out into traffic. "Vinyl, dude. Quit hating on the ride." Brian's mood had shifted into survival mode as he both tore into his sandwich and kept his eyes on the road. "Good call on the vittles, by the way."

"Can't beat the Big Montana. Plain, though."

"Definitely plain. Best big sandwich for driving, too."

"I was thinking about the Super, but-"

"-absolutely not. Lettuce and tomato on roast beef? I don't think so. And what the hell is that red sauce? Naw, you did well, Jay. Just mind the foil." For about three days after each Bullet detail Brian was particularly anal about clutter.

"Yes sir. Shit, I'll bet that's Bill. Damn if I didn't forget to call," I said, straightening my legs to get the vibrating cell out of my pocket. "Yup. Bildo."

"Why don't you get a clip for the damn thing? Or do you want people to think it's part of your package? 'Is that a phone in your pocket, or are you..."

"...shhhhhello? Hey Dad." I never let on that I knew it was him that was calling, by answering the phone with the 'hey Dad' part first, because I'd tried that a few times, and I spent way too long each time explaining how I knew it was him. I was better off just acting surprised. "Sir? With Brian Dildy. Yes, Dad, one of *those* three." Brian made a face like the guy on Munch's *The Scream*, or like McCauley Caulkin in *Home Alone* if you're not as learned. "Sir? I did tell you. This morning. All evening. Very late. Sir? Who called? Why would Mr. Markowski call you?"

"Shit," Brian suddenly, distractedly whispered.

"I know," I returned, covering the phone.

"No, man, shit. The police, man. FuckI'mbeingpulledgodDAMmit." Brian's eyes were stuck to the rearview. "Gotta get off and help me man. FuckfuckfuckFUCK." He slapped Roz.

I held one finger up to Brian, *hold on a second*. "No Dad, I have no idea. None. Dad, I gotta... sir? Well, I'll think on it and we'll talk tomorrow. It'll be too late tonight. Dad, I gotta, yes, I'll be fine. I know I have SAT class tomorrow. Early, I know.

"Shitfuckpiss," Brian said through clenched teeth, flicking on his directional, keeping both hands at ten and two, looking back and forth over his right shoulder for a good time to switch lanes as if he were back in driver's ed.

"Dad, really, please, I'll listen to his message when I get homeIreallygottagoloveyabye."

My legs got weak when I finally saw the blue and white lights in my side mirror as Brian pulled to the curb, and I too cursed Rocinante for being so clean because there was no place to camouflage our sippees.

Poor Roz. None of this was her fault.

"Got any gum, man? Mints or something?" I reached again into my pockets and pulled out some Arby's after dinner candies they had in a display bowl by the register, the ones in the white wrappers with *Arby's* in red on the side. "Here." I quickly unwrapped him four. "Suck fast, dude." I grabbed his sippee, and mine, and again straightened my legs to stuff them down the front of my pants. Cold beer shot up through the straws onto my belly and into my crotch as the cups bent when I sat. I loosely untucked my shirt to cover the bulge and the stain.

"If I get out of this I will be forever loyal to the Big Montana. Maybe even write her an ode." Brian crunched and sucked on all four mints, looking in his rearview as we sat on the shoulder, cars slowing as they passed in both directions for a chance to spread some news.

"Good thing she's a Taurus, huh? Plenty of those around." Brian tapped on his steering wheel and glanced now into his side view mirror. "Pick up that foil, Jay, the one by your feet." I'd never seen the guy so nervous.

"Brian, I can't move. I've got about 24 ounces shoved in my waistline and six more soaking my balls."

"Good thing your dad called when he did." Brian tittered. "What a shocker, huh, the phone in your pocket? Bzzzzzz. Actually, sounds kind of kinky okay here he comes. Just chill man. I'll talk." He straightened up.

"Don't talk too much," I said quickly. Brian unrolled the window.

"License and registration."

"Of course," Brian stammered, leaning across me to the glove compartment. "Forgot that part." The officer bent down with his arm on the hood and stared across at me, at the floors, at the back seat. "Here you go, sir. Sorry for the wait. What seems to be the problem?" Brian had rehearsed that one.

"Reason for the pull's your left tail light's busted." The officer examined Brian's information.

"Fucking Silver Bullet."

"Sir?" The officer's voice inflected a bit as he leaned down to face Brian.

"Officer, I'm sorry. Just that the car was just detailed and before that the light was fine. Got some people to talk to, is all."

"I see. Okay, then, Mr., uh, Dildy. Daddy's name Pete?"

Jeremy Stevens

"No sir. Pete's my uncle. Always called him Uncle Petey, though haven't been out to their place in a while since Skip moved away. Skip, that's his son, my cousin."

Sweet Jesus.

"Alright, Mr. Dildy, just sit tight while I check on this information here."

The officer walked back to his car and Brian let his head fall against the steering wheel. "Fucking hate my last name. Dil-dy. One fucking vowel away from a vibrating sex toy."

"Dude, the name might actually help you here. You did go a bit far, though, with your life, like the cop hadn't seen you since you were this tall. You might have ended with, 'Pete's my uncle.' Period."

"Jay, now's the time to boost the ol' morale, ya know? Not bring it down, dammit."

"You're right. Sorry. Just don't fucking talk so much. You've been drinking, and those are only Arby's mints. Probably don't have that Retsyn shit."

Brian just stared into the rearview, repeating "fuck" as if to ward off evil spirits.

"Man, check this out," I continued, trying to lighten the mood. "If I had your last name, my dad would be Bildo Dildy."

Brian remained expressionless. "Yea, funny." Still staring into the rearview, he continued in monotone, as if hypnotized. "Bet *that's* why she left. Who'd want to inherit 'Dildy' for a last name, to give birth to 2.5 little Dildys? I'll wind up one of those pussies who takes the woman's last name. Dude, reality is I'll never find another G."

While Premier did have its national recognition for SAT performance and university acceptance, it was seriously lacking in chib talent. Woe betide the transfer or foreign exchange student with even a modicum of femininity, for she was in for some hard-core appraisal rivaling hell week in any college sorority.

I was a sophomore when Gabrielle Marceau began her senior study abroad from Paris, and "studying a broad" was precisely what every guy within calling distance of "her league" did; until, finally, perhaps out of exasperation, perhaps out of fear, or perhaps simply out of curiosity, she said *yes* to Brian.

Word was the proposals were numerous and varied, from personal to telephone to letter, to everything from dinner and a movie to bowling and bingo.

Brian, also a senior and definitely a contender, patiently played the stoic observer while they lined up and were summarily shot down.

Recognizing my own limitations, I just ogled from afar.

"Jayman, I'm gonna land that French chib," Brian said offhandedly one day at lunch between very full bites of rib-b-que. I'd never heard of girls being referred to as "chiblets" until I met Brian. He used the term frequently.

"Bet," I said. "Mighty Taco after the airstrip this Friday."

"Done," and with that he got up, brushed his hands together, tossed his trash, and with unparalleled confidence walked to Gabrielle's very crowded table with nothing but a casual wave to my incredulous *what, NOW?!*

Though I'd been hanging with the guy only a few weeks, Brian Dildy was everything I wanted to be. He was good looking, cool, funny as hell, casual, and true to a fault. He was very smart in things that interested him, and did just enough to get by in things that didn't, and he didn't bat an eyelash at a D. *Gives me lots of room to improve*, he'd say. *People love a fucking success story.* He liked everyone, and you couldn't help but like him back.

Brian Dildy, in my mind, was perfect.

Not two minutes later he returned, shaking a carton of chocolate milk and whistling *I Dream of Genie*. I stared at him over my tray of untouched Italian-style goulash, allowing Brian his time to digest, knowing our reactions were being gauged for hi-fives and/or the geek dance, two certain eliminations from any would-be score.

"Are they still looking?" he finally asked.

"Nope. Actually, they're all leaving except the one-armed Korean girl."

"Yea, she's the spy." Brian downed his milk in one swallow.

"So she bit?"

"Jay," Brian sighed, shaking his head, and continued with mournful erudition. "Jay, you simply do not ask a cultured French woman as Gabrielle Marceau to a Hugh Grant romance or to dinner at The Olive Garden, or to Rollerworks to skate for Christ's sake. No, no, no. These boys. They're just so damn *American*."

"Soooo, she bit, then."

"You're darn tootin' she bit." He slammed his hand on the table. "Jay, my cup runneth over. Friday night I get piss-drunk with my best friend at the airstrip, followed by a complimentary #5 meat, bean, and cheese super supreme deluxe combo, biggie size on everything, and on Saturday afternoon it's to the pond to feed the ducks with the Premier Parisian."

"Ducks?"

"Well, geese actually. Ducks and geese. Are you kidding, Jay? Hand-feeding all those soft, cuddly little innocent fowl? We'll be betrothed by sundown. Dig this, though, man. I saw it on the Food Network.

"You're gonna eat the cute ducks, Bri?

"No, man. See, it's called *pate'*, dude. It's all subliminal. The French, they just love some fat geese."

I didn't see too much of Brian during the eighteen months he dated Gabrielle, and I was able to focus virtually undistractedly on my studies, which rejuvenated Father's hope for his budding protégé. After graduation, Gabrielle extended her visa and the two got an apartment together, Brian to work and continue his schooling, and Gabby, as he affectionately called her, to waitress at Applebee's. The two vowed their eternal love for each other through monogrammed tattoos. Brian had a **G**, entwined by a red rose vine, emblazoned on his right bicep; Gabrielle, a و̂ (she insisted it was a Japanese "B") on her left ass cheek.

Brian thought "Hentai," and loved her even more.

The steamy romance ended and Brian's heart broke when he found his Gabby in bed with the restaurant's fry cook. Matters were made worse and Brian's torment was fed when he learned that the guy's name was Bob, he was of some Asian descent, and that it wasn't the first time.

And all Brian could deduce was that neither the tattoo, nor her ass, were ever really his.

4. A Blessing or a Curse

"Mr. Dildy, had anything to drink this afternoon?" Lightly slapping Brian's information in the palm of his hand, the officer was eerily casual in the way he posed the question, as if he were either trying to strike up conversation or simply biding time.

"Sir?" Brian asked, obviously having heard the question, but trying to bide his own time in return to formulate a clever answer.

The officer, he just stared with a furrowed brow as if to say *you heard me the first time, son*. Brian sighed heavily and looked down. "Yes. Yessir, I have."

"I see." The officer paused in thought. "Do you still live at 23 Clarendon?"

"Yessir. Just right down the road. You could probably hit my apartment if-"

"-okay, Mr. Dildy. It's very important now," the officer interrupted, a bit impatiently and with pointed finger, "that you tuck away every word you are about to hear, because this could either be a blessing or a curse, depending upon how *you* want to play it." Brian blew a heavy, long breath with puffed cheeks. He could do that now, with the officer knowing he'd been drinking.

"Your honesty, Mr. Dildy, has saved you a potentially long evening and an even longer sentence, and while I believe in the law I also am a firm believer in second chances. This is yours."

Brian nodded. "Yes sir," with emphasis on the *sir*.

"I am going to follow you back to, uh," the officer glanced down at the license, "23 Clarendon, and I strongly advise you not to drive again this evening. Do you understand?"

"Yessir. Yes, I do. I do."

"Mr. Dildy, I am certain you will not make me regret my decision this afternoon."

"No sir. No. I will make you proud, Officer Cruz." I rolled my eyes.

The officer handed Brian his information, and Brian tossed it on my lap. We drove the quarter mile to his apartment in complete silence, and even after we parked and the officer continued on---I was thinking there'd be a toot of the horn or a wave or something, but no---we sat, anchored in Roz while she coughed and sputtered, glad to be home.

"Dude, what just happened?" Brian finally asked, still staring at the same nothing I'd been fixed on. "What just happened, Jay?" he repeated, turning to me. "You were there."

I shook my head and freed the dented sippees, phewing relief as my waistline depressurized while shifting uncomfortably in the now lukewarm overflow. I handed Brian his. "Here," I said, and unlocked my door.

"Jason."

"What?"

"Your, thoughts, dude."

"Brian, shit. I don't know what just happened, man. Nice cop. It's your lucky day. There is a God. Dildy's an awesome last name, wish it were mine. I don't fucking know." I collapsed into the headrest. "It always seems to work out for you, Brian. I'm really happy for you."

"You're acting as if you wish it hadn't."

"No, 'Bill,' I'm not, dammit. I'm acting like I'm drunk, like I have swamp ass, and like I have some explaining to do to my father who, by the way, received a call from my sociology teacher, and who I hung up on not twenty minutes ago. For Christ's sake, don't hold me accountable too, alright?" I took three long pulls from the straw; the beer, while a bit flat, was surprisingly cool. "Actually, come to think of it, I'm not drunk a bit. Cruz musta scared it out of me." I finished the thermos with a loud slurp.

"OK, son," Brian chuckled. "How's it taste?"

"Manna from heaven."

"I'll bet. Come on, boy. Let's get you some fresh drawers."

5. Dinner

I kept a change or two of clean clothes at Brian's for the frequent Friday or Saturday nights I crashed at his crib, or for the late afternoons I spilled beer down my crotch.

Brian and I did not share drawers. I don't think even chicks do that.

Having showered and changed into what I planned to wear to the party that evening--- boot-cut, frayed-end jeans; a partially-untucked oxford; a $17 tee shirt and black loafers, all part of a Banana Republic look I adopted from Brian---I claimed the recliner and the remote and surfed his two hundred-plus channels with two fresh, very cold bottles of Samuel Adams. I didn't want to have to get up any time soon.

"Call Jed n' Chat?" I hollered in to Brian, who was washing vegetables in the sink for the stir fry.

By the standards you'd expect from a typical twenty-year-old bachelor, Brian was excellent in the kitchen, and actually enjoyed reading and experimenting from easy to follow cookbooks, from the original *Joy of Cooking* to *Emeril's Cooking with Power*. There was a time I thought he did it for the score factor, and he probably did because it *is* unique in a man and considered sexy, I'd heard; however, it definitely grew on him, as now he actually considers anything Kraft a "blight on humanity," and keeps the freezer solely for his late-night drunk menu.

Shit, the man not only owned but used a stainless steel asparagus steamer.

In fact, Brian really was an anomaly. With the help from a bi-monthly cleaning lady named Betty, Brian kept his apartment every day the way he kept Roz the few days or so after her detail; again, because the ladies were partial to cleanliness, but also again because Brian grew to prefer domestic hygiene over filth.

Where Betty took care of the finer details like dust, grout, film, and lime, Brian maintained the superficial order of bed making, dish washing, plant watering; and eventually, the cataloguing of his broad expanse of CD's, DVD's, and Playstation 4 and Wii video games, because he discovered that if he didn't, Betty would, and they would not be found.

The purpose of the doormat was for the placement of shoes, not for wiping them; the hand towels in the bathroom were for decoration, as were the tri-colored sea shelled bars of soap in the dish. (Hence, the steel wire paper towel holder and the decorative liquid soap dispenser on the sink.)

In my life, I'd say I'd met two latent homosexuals. One played Tony in the school's musical *West Side Story*, opposite a well-endowed, absolutely smoking brunette who was an outside audition for Maria but who nonetheless made theater-goers of the majority population of our male student body. The second was a cheerleader who supported, nightly, 110 lbs. of spread skirt above his head. Naturally, I dubbed them both potentially gay because of their octaves, theater make-up, skips, prances and pom-poms.

But, they *were* always around women; and, though I would never deign to admit it, maybe, just *maybe*, there was that chance they were not gay, and that in the end they eventually got the score.

One visit to Brian's apartment, without knowing Brian, and you'd entertain the same thoughts about him. Absolutely. However, Brian's being slightly in touch with his feminine side was fine by me as I was the primary beneficiary of his eccentricities.

So long as it remained "slightly."

"Bri, did you call Jed n'...."

"I'm in the kitchen, Jason," he shouted back over the running water and sizzling wok, implying as a parent would how I needed to proceed with the conversation.

I was beginning to get a little bit impatient with the evening thus far. The television had lots to offer anyone interested in extreme wrestling, virtual lives, bad news, or big tits, and while *Sponge Bob* had seen me through my first beer and a half I caught it half way through and *Danny Phantom* sucked. My father was renting space in my head and I was trying desperately to flush out him and that call from Markowski, but it simply was not working. I was getting bloated on beer and wanted nothing of Brian's stir-fried anything.

I wanted out.

I wanted to shoot Absinthe intravenously, to snort Everclear.

Nothing gradual, nothing social.

I wanted release, I wanted deviance.

I wanted hard liquor; I wanted grunge.

"Man, I gotta tell ya," I began, slumping in the barstool at the kitchen counter, "Bill never should have called. It's like the man..."

"...if you mention that fucking name one more time tonight I am really going to have to kick your ass. Now here, try this." Expecting a fork-full of beef and bamboo shoots I was surprised, a bit spooked in fact, to be handed a shot glass of clear liquid, as if my friend had extrasensory perception.

"Vodka?"

"Drink it," Brian said using his Fats Williams bar patron impression from *Weird Science*.

I tossed it back and down, and immediately I thought of rubbing astringent I put on scrapes as a child and I just *knew* Brian had chosen this over kicking my ass. My eyes welled with tears and I gasped at its putrescence and I stared at the wicked, wicked man in front of me, who just smiled knowingly and said, "Now, this," and I grabbed the fork-full of beef and bamboo shoots and sucked its spice and heat and swallowed it whole as if it were antivenin.

It was the perfect foil. The student had become the teacher.

"Cheap Korean liquor. You like?"

"Absolutely not."

Jeremy Stevens

"Good. I'd worry about you if you did. Here, then," and he handed me a plate of stir fry and another beer and sat across from me. "Eat up, young Patawan. You'll need your energy."

"What was that?" I asked, grabbing the bottle. Soju. Never heard of it. "Never heard of it," I told Brian. Suddenly, I wanted stir fry. Lots and lots of Brian's stir fry. I poured myself another shot. "You?"

"Yea, but we should take it easy on the stuff. It's like 80 proof and apparently leaves a killer hangover, though the Korean men say it produces stamina so perhaps it's worth the trade, depending on how hard up you are."

"Pretty damn hard up." I slammed back my third shot and chased it with spice. "Only thing needed now is to hear some Rage, or Alice, man, to set the pace."

"Nah, dude. Too many senses at work. Just chill with the silence." Brian was using chop sticks and was sitting up straight, proper. "Besides," he continued as an afterthought, "couldn't provide anyhow, I don't think. Betty's done some rearranging. Can't find a damn thing."

There was a very faint ringing in my ears and my body felt cocooned and warmly numb and my arm moved mechanically from plate to mouth, almost involuntarily, and I was comfortable in that straight-backed bar chair as if it were an orthopedic contour fit, like a "sleep number" chair. Brian was right. Music would have been a complete distraction.

"When reading up on the stuff I learned that Korea just passed legislation allowing all alcohol-related accidents to be covered by workplace insurance. Sure says something about a problem, doncha think? Jay?"

My face was buried in food. I was only half listening to Cliff Claven from *Cheers* sitting across from me, spilling out periodic "little known facts" as I shoveled it down. I floated to the kitchen to help myself to more.

"Fantastic compliment to the chef, Jason. Silence and seconds. You are my biggest fan."

Indeed I was. Without question or contest, Brian Dildy was at the center of my universe. Brian, his stir fry, and his liquor.

6. Fading In

Chat is playing preacher again.

Chat always preaches when he's smoked his funny stuff.

Jed had probably smoked too because he is silently absorbed in *Dog: Bounty Hunter*, sitting anesthetized, motionless, a foot away from the screen.

I have no clue how long they've been here, or what I was doing when they arrived, or why I am carrying the half-drunk bottle of Soju, or how much of it I drank, or why I am wearing Brian's football helmet or what the hell music is playing.

I just sort of faded in, just now.

Chat: (*talking to Brian*) See man, Dilbert, check it out. Tonight, case in point. All's I got to do is raise my voice a bit, and start speaking with my hands and arms and shit, like this, and guarangoddamtee ya I'll be center stage, man. Watch.

Brian: Jed, shoes dude. Shoes at the door. Simplest shit ever.

Chat: Brian, *I* got the conch, man. (*Chat liked "Lord of the Flies," even more so because he actually finished it. He uses that line when it's his turn to speak.*) It's my turn to speak. So, suddenly I'll be surrounded by a flock of little Eminems named Austin and Houston, throwin' up hands'n sayin' "bling" and "dawg" and shit.

Brian: (*mindlessly bouncing quarters into a I Got Shot Up at Dick's shotglass*) Preach the word, Charles. (*Then, to me*) Jayman, change this shit dude. (*I remember now that I had played* Der Kommissar *at some point and never pressed stop, never put in a new disc.*) Put in some Snoop for the Reverend Charles.

Jed: *Doggystyle*, track three Jaydude. "Rollin down the street, smokin' indo, sippin'on gin and juice, laid back." (*The back of Jed's head is nodding rhythmically. That is all.*)

Chat: (*to Brian*) That's "Chat," asshole, and look. While Cody and Tyler play wigger, Molly and Anna Blair will be gigglin' and whisperin' over there in the corner, wonderin' if it's true what they say.

Brian: JED!

Jed: Alright, alright. Damn. *(Jed pries off his Timberlands with his heels.)* Feet smell like Doritos, Bri, gonna have to get some Plug Ins now.

Me: Why don't you just go by Charles? *(The helmet makes my voice as tunneled as my vision.)* Charlie Parker was a really cool black cat. We could call you "Bird."

Chat: You ever meet a black guy named Charles Parker who didn't wear argyle, professor? *(Chat always calls me professor.)*

Brian: *(attempting quickly to speak between cough and sputter and swallow of his beer, the foam of which now runs down his bottle).* Put that back, Jed. *(Brian is running to the sink to catch the beer. Jed is pointing the remote to the television a foot away from the screen.)* Move your melon, dude. *(Jed has to move again to allow for our view of Jessica Alba on the E! channel.)* Hot chiblet. H-O-T. Perfect chick-super hero in Fantastic Four.

Me: *(to no one in particular)* Who's the hottest cartoon chick?

Chat: The bitch on the Rumpleminz label.

Me: *(after staring at Chat quizzically for a few seconds)* No, uh, dude. No. Television-or-movie-hot-cartoon-chick.

Chat: *(to no one in particular)* Why do White boys always speak like they in the wild west with that "dude" shit?

Brian: I'll bite, Jay. *(He finishes his beer in pause)* Meg, from *Hercules*.

Jed: *(suddenly interested in communication, going to the refrigerator)* Naw dude, too much hair. You wanna go Disney, go Jasmine in *Aladdin*.

Chat: Ariel, *Little Mermaid*.

Jed: Mrs. Incredible. Bri, where's the opener?

Me: Super hero chicks don't count. They're all hot. Besides, that's Pixar and she's a mom.

Jed: Shows she puts out, 'least.

Brian: Judy Jetson.

Chat: Pebbles Flintstone.

Me: The correct answer is D, none of the above. I got you all. Brian, drumroll. *(I take off the helmet so I can pound the beer in front of me, though I have no idea whose it is. It is warm and flat.)* The hottest cartoon chick ever is, bar none, Jessica Rabbit. *(And with that it all rises,* *furiously, the beer and the Big Montana and the beer and the pounds of beef and bamboo and the Soju and the unknown beer. I throw down the helmet and I run to the bathroom.)*

Chat: Damn. Never thought of her.

Brian: Jessica Rabbit. That sunuvagun.

Jed: Yes, indeed. Our little Jay, all grown up.

And Chat, Brian, and Jed all toast my victory and drink up while I pray hard over the bowl until, however much time has elapsed, it is time to go to the party.

7. Greta and Hillary

"Oh-my-God. Is it? Is it?"

"Hey Hill." The two gave tight, one-armed hugs, cheeks pressed together with wide smiles---*mmmm*--- and Hillary got in the car completely and shut the door.

"It is. I am still *so* not believing this." Hillary began digging for the mascara in the bottom of her small evening purse crammed full of everything from her day purse, so full the teeth had to be pinched together before it would zipper. "I truly thought I'd never see this day again." She pulled the visor down for the mirror. The two drove away.

"Believe it, girl."

"I mean, no, stop. Let me look at you-"

"-I can't just *stop*-"

"-you know what I mean. Just pose a sec." Greta flashed a quick Maybelline smile, and Hillary leaned back for the full-body and clicked a pretend camera. "Damn I wish I had your genes." Hillary shook her head and began fumbling again.

"Damn I wish I had *yours*. Diesel?"

"You're too kind."

"But the shoes-"

"-now the shoes *are* Pucci." She stretched her legs to look at her feet.

Jeremy Stevens

"Ka-*yute*. And I love your hair."

"Do you? I don't know yet." Hillary scratched her scalp like she had a bad itch. "Eddie likes me in auburn."

"Gay Eddie should know."

"There isn't much my sweet little Mexican man doesn't know about me, sitting in his chair for two hours. I wish all men showed such interest."

"Tell me about it." Greta looked behind her to switch lanes.

"No, you."

"What?"

"*What*, what. I heard your tone."

"What tone?"

"Your 'he's-gone-and-done-it-again' tone. It's been a while, darling, but I still know the tone."

"It hasn't been that long-"

"-just spill it, chick. There's a reason we're going out tonight, and it isn't because you've missed me so. Though I do still love you."

Greta sighed and pulled into the next parking lot. "Wanna Frosty?"

"Diet-something, sweetie," said Hillary. "Frosty's the reason I don't wear Diesel."

They sat at a two-top on the drive-thru side, Greta with a Frosty and Hillary with double bacon cheeseburger combo, diet Coke. They had no real plans before the party in the Country Club other than Hillary needed to be picked up by eight or her mother would find something else for her to do, so Wendy's was first, then the mall at some point because that's what they'd always done in the life before Tommy.

"I'm pretty sure he's sleeping around."

"What makes you think that, other than the obvious?"

"What's the obvious?"

"Like, *duh*. The man's only a complete hunk, he makes over seventy grand, and he drives a convertible Audi, candy apple red. The car alone says 'fuck me.'"

"Hillary!"

"Well Jesus, Greta, what do you want? For me to say, 'No, sweetie, it's all in your head'?"

"I know, I kn-"

"-it wasn't just the *jealous* best friend shooting warning flares when you first met him at, hmmmm, let me remember..."

"Roxy's."

"Roxy's. That's right. And where is he tonight, pray tell?"

"Satisfactions."

"Right. A Roxy's, but without the clothes. Perfectly innocent."

"It's not like he's just *going*, going. It's a bachelor party."

"Swine."

"I know, I know. But tonight's not why I think he's cheating."

"Sure as hell doesn't help." Hillary put some fries in her burger. They tasted better like that at Wendy's, she said.

Greta stirred her Frosty with a long handled spoon. "Tommy hit me last night." Hillary stopped in mid-chew. Her brow furrowed. "I answered his cell when he was in the shower and a bubbly little voice said to tell him Katie called."

Hillary swallowed. "And when you did?"

Greta mouthed out a smooth even round top of the dessert on her spoon. "And when I did, he punched me in the stomach and told me never to answer his effin' phone again."

"Only he didn't say 'effin'."

"No, no, he said The Word."

Hillary was about to say The Word, but Tommy had soiled it. "Damn, Greta."

"Yeah. Damn. And to think I was actually going to get a tattoo of his initials. Not now. No way."

"You got a pierce for him, though."

"But down *there*, Hill, where Daddy won't ever see. But T I T on the lower back side would be a bit harder to explain. To anyone."

"T I T?"

"His initials. Tommy Isaac Thomas. Believe me, he loves his initials."

"Damn, Greta," Hillary chuckled, and took the bun off to load some more fries. "Have you told Carlie?" Carlie was Greta's roommate a Brinkley University.

"Carlie's home for the weekend. And besides...oh, I don't know."

"Talk."

"It's just that, Hill, you're the one I need to be sharing this stuff with, not Carlie. And I've pretty much ex'd you out, since Tommy, that is."

"Apology accepted, and I said I still love you. Now eat your Frosty. It might help ease *my* guilt a bit."

The shops were beginning to pull the metal grates over their fronts and the canned hypnotic malltunes had been turned off and Saks especially was not last-minute accommodating of the two flitty socialite-wannabe's who were making wish lists, "just looking, thank you."

It was nearing 10:00 and the two now sat in the car. Greta just assumed they got on, though Hillary thought it was still too early and the only people at the party now would be those who had curfews.

"We could go back to Brinkley, watch some TV in the student union," suggested Greta. "They have karaoke, too, I think, on Friday nights."

"Or better yet, we could have ourselves a little party outside the party." The joint Hillary produced from that crowded little purse had somehow maintained its perfect shape: a fat, white paper toothpick, wrinkle and tear-free.

It startled Greta, and she looked around. "It sure has been a while," she said with uncertainty about her own merits.

"And I'm sure Tommy would absolutely *hate* it," said Hillary.

"I'm sure he would, the weenie."

"Such language."

They bought some whisky cocktail splashers and drove to the Country Club, and though the cars would have indicated a party in progress they sat on a curb. They drank and they smoked; and as their mood warmed they said *hey* to random guys, and girls, some of whom helped form a circle, around which they passed the roach freely.

Hillary began digging yet again through her purse, this time for a nickel bag she knew she'd brought, and some rolling papers; and giggling, she handed Greta a condom. "Ribbed, for her pleasure," she said with a howl, and the two of them fell back in the thick grass and laughed. "My gift, to you."

Greta held the small square package above her face against the leafy canopy and star specks. She felt so comfortable, lying back in that thick grass.

Like it was meant for her.

The night, face up.

"Fuck you, Tommy-Isaac-Thomas," she declared to the condom.

"There you go, girl. Fuck him."

And Hillary said The Word into the night.

8. Brian's "G"

"Dilbert, I'm having a really hard time believin' you straight up told the cop you'd been drinkin' when he asked, 'Son, you been drinkin?' Natural inclination'd be to lie, dude, or to say 'one, off'cer, only had one.'" Jed held up his pointer finger in demonstration.

"That, Jed dear, is what sep'rates man from beast, me from you. I go by reason, you by your 'natural inclination.' Where I question why there's a fresh cube of Swiss on a brass spring, you think a nibble might be nice."

Brian and I were in the back of Chat's souped-up Camry. We all had to yell over the bass of something-rap that made the windows

Jeremy Stevens

vibrate. The explosion in Brian's toilet had eased my drunk quite a bit; the others, well, I didn't know, only that Jed and Chat were passing a bowl up front and I thought it was an exceptionally bad idea, especially with the vibrating windows.

"Where *I*," directing his point now towards the back of Chat's head and shouting even louder, "conceal my beverage in a strawed thermos and at least *attempt* disguise through mints, you not only smoke your shit with all the windows up but you ten-dial it like we're in fuckin' Compton."

Glad to know Brian had not only his reason, but his senses as well.

"Bri's right, dude," Jed turned to Chat.

"What, that you an animal?" Chat yelled back. "How many I times I tole' you that?"

"Fuckin' amateurs," Brian leaned back. "So long as we're not smokin' that shit, we're okay, I guess. Just along for the ride. Innocent. Glad I didn't bring that beer, though it's positively criminal to leave behind a full beer to soften. I oughta be ashamed. I oughta be ashamed, right Jay?" He shook my shoulder hard; I exaggeratedly rocked back and forth. "Love ya, dude. Mean it. Jessica Rabbit. Priceless, Jay." I could tell by his flow of words that Brian was looped, but he was still pretty much the same guy.

"You okay, though, right Jayman?"

I did feel remarkably well, like I could even drink some more. "Yeah. Sorry about wasting your dinner, though. I know you put a lot of effort into it."

"Dude, once it's down the hatch I consider it sold. 'Less, of course, you're bulimic. Then it's Stouffer's for your ass. Really glad you're okay, though. Was worried about you a bit, though it'd been worse if you kept the helmet on, I guess." Jed offered back the bowl, probably knowing we'd both decline but felt it proper to do so anyhow, just so he could follow up with his "more for me" line and his stoner giggle. Brian never smoked anything, probably a result of athletics in school, and he had a label for those who did, "slacker pothead" and the like. As I did not enjoy labels, especially from my best friend, I did not toke up around him. It wasn't worth it.

"Really, though, dude, to give Jed a bit of credit, how did you know to tell the truth? I think I'da probally lied too with that *only one, officer* bit. Does seem like a natural reaction. 'Least it gives you a chance."

"Jay, I applaud your integrity. I liken Jedidiah to a quadruped, and you amble aboard the 'ol Ark right next to him. Real fiber, you got." He called it "taking the right angle instead of the hypotenuse," his gift of the gab, building up suspense for the punch line regardless of how trivial.

"See, it's like this," and I recognized his impersonation immediately. "If a cop has to ask you if you've been drinking, he already knows. Any drunk scuzzbag who lies to an officer of the law has already signed 'guilty' on the dotted line of justice. It'll be out of the frying pan and into a jail cell for that bozo."

"That wildest police videos show, right?"

"They're all Fox reruns now, and John Bunnell *is* total cheese with his teeth and silver hair, but sometimes he tosses out something I can store for later."

"Hamburgers, hotdogs, apple pie, and baseball. America has given the world many things, including high speed pursuits."

"'Zactly, Jay. Nicely done. Guy's a fuckin' gem."

Chat tossed back the folded, crinkled directions that looked like they'd been through the wash, or in his back pocket for over a week. 1. Go to Country Club. 2. Look for cars. They were written at the top of some notes he had scribbled down while reeling in a potential telemarketing client, the same client he lost when his cell phone rang with the directions.

Telemarketing 101: The general public's reaction to being put on hold by a telemarketer is probably not a favorable one.

It took Chat ten minutes to narrow the Camry between two mammoth eight-seaters. I thought it better to drive about a hundredth of a mile down the road, to the near-end of the long line of luxury automobiles; but Chat, doggedly fixed on his present challenge, would hear nothing of it from a back-seater.

Brian, seeing too this could be a while, resumed conversation. "Gonna find my G tonight, Jayman. Just feel it." He tossed this out between attempting to guide Chat in---*left, dude, hard left now*---and craning his neck in ridiculous positions to catch every angle.

Jed finally turned the music down and wheeled around in the front seat to face us. "You still on that shit, Brian? Why don't you just suck it up and get the damned tat removed?" A reverb pulsated in my head. I needed air.

"Because it's boss and I don't have the money, and I heard the area looks worse after and that they can't remove red anyhow."

"So you're gonna hold out for a girl whose name begins with a G, is that it? Good, Chat, stop. Stop dude, your wheels are rubbin'." Chat stopped and fumbled for his door handle.

"You all stay here," he tried. "I'm gonna check."

"Fuck that, dude, I'm out," Brian said, taking charge and opening his door. I followed, and Jed scurried out his side. *Catch up when you get it straightened out* seemed to be our parting advice to Chat, though I don't think he realized we had gone, he was that absorbed in the parallel park.

"Not 'hold out,' dude, like celibacy or anything," Brian continued as we proceeded down the center of the oak-lined road towards where we presumed the party was being held. "Just not commit to. I'll always be a member of the species, for Christ's sake."

"I once got flowers from this chib named....um.....well, name's not important," Jed said. "Anyhow, I turned around and gave those flowers to this other babe I was trying to bed." We began to hear a faint cacophony of music and voices. Couples were leaning against cars. Small groups sat whispering in curb-side circles, an orange dot passing between them like a curious insect. A girl from one group said "hey." We said *hey* back.

"Shoulda checked for a card first. Point is, Bri, that there isn't a chick alive who'd dig a second-hand tattoo."

"Actually, that's where you're wrong, Jed," I contributed. I skipped along excitedly, hands deep in my pockets. "I'm sure the geriatric wing has plenty of lonely ladies. There's Gladys, and Grace, and---oooooh!---there's Gertrude. You could call her Gertie, Bri."

"Alright, shitbird, enough outta you," Brian said playfully, and like an older brother got me in a headlock. "Say 'Goliath.' G-G-Goliath, Skippy. Say it."

"Goliath!" The reduced oxygen to my head and the bouncing quickly pronounced the drunk I thought I was losing yet again that evening. Brian let go. "Goliath, Mr. Dildo San."

"Right," and with that he pushed me to the ground, he lay on top of me, and he counted down as if to declare a pin in wrestling. My face felt smeared with lawn, yet still I laughed. "Hell of a name for a woman, Bri. Goliath. Where ya gonna find her, the fuckin' carnival?"

He helped me up. "C'mon, boy, time to drink. You're getting sober; you know not what you say."

The house was directly in front of us. Every light was on and there were moving silhouettes behind the curtains; however, despite the quantity of cars and the likewise many, many would-be-untamed guests, the celebration was surprisingly muffled.

"'Sides, man, I love you. I *want* it to hurt me more than you when I have to dish you a Goliath ass-whoopin'," and again he pushed me, though this time I didn't fall. I chased him the rest of the way, over the moat to the castle door.

9. The Party

The house was what you'd expect of people who "summered" anywhere: six thousand square feet of red brick on three acres near the

Jeremy Stevens

ninth hole; black walnut floors; cathedral and vaulted ceilings; private baths in all four bedrooms; a game room with everything from pool and Ping-Pong tables, a plasma HDTV with 3D, and a full stereo component system with Dolby surround to skylights, leather upholstery, and a well-padlocked wet bar; granite countertops in a stainless-steel sterile kitchen; an intercom system; a triple attached garage with a Navigator, an Audi, and a Bentley with a vanity plate that said MDLFCRSIS; an Olympic-style in-ground pool, and a Shitzu.

Enter, friend. Now, who are you?
I've seen your face a time or two.
Chess club champ? FBLA?
Please note the sign: Children at Play.
Lose the vest, dude, have a toke,
just sit back in that chair and smoke.
Here's a shot, it's Jim Beam Black.
Now quick, this beer to knock it back.
Sunshine daydream, midnight blue.
The keg's quite full, we've work to do.
Moderation is the key,
but you came late. Catch up to me!
Pound it down, now, hard and fast.
You're quite impressive, can you last?
Fermentation, purple haze,
another spleef for life's malaise.
Cotton-mouthed, another beer,
wow, you look great! When'd you get here?
Would you like a glass of wine?
I've never seen you look so fine.
Who's your friend? Have you lost weight?
'Greta,' you say? It must be fate.

"Greta?"
"Greta."

"She hot?"

"Think so."

"Dude, you been smokin' some funny stuff?"

"Depends."

"Depends upon what?"

"De Pen's upon de desk, next to de pencil." I had just made that up. I laughed, and I sounded like a kid firing his make-believe machine gun.

"Dude, that sucked and you're high. And your laugh, it sucks too."

I hung my head and bounced it a bit. "It did, and I am, and it does. Bad, bad Jason. Bad boy. Bad."

"Alright, stoner dude, look. It's 12:30 and if I'm gonna land this 'Greta' chib I'll need to see some paperwork. What's she drinkin'?"

"Vodka Red Bull. But Bri, dudeman, listen for a sec, okay? 'Cause I'm, I'm sorry, man. I'm sorry, ya know?" I looked at him, eyes dry as if they'd been propped open in a wind tunnel. "You are my best friend, there, Bri, and I don't want you disappointed in me. You know what I mean?"

The sincerity in Brian's voice that followed might have been refreshing for one who thought him incapable of anything serious. Indeed, Brian was laid back, perhaps at times a bit too carefree about the relative "small stuff," but I'll say it again: Brian was true, and when he said he loved you, the way guys can love each other, he meant it.

"Jason Ottomar Braswell, I am a drunk individual, and you know what they say about wine and truth so this should mean a whole lot to you." He had his arm draped around my shoulders and was leaning closely to my ear, as if for support but really to be heard over the din of something-reggae, for rarely had I ever seen Brian truly unbalanced, truly unglued.

He was a dangerous drunk, because unless you knew him as well as I did, or unless he told you, measuring his inebriety was difficult.

"You told me before not to hold you accountable, and with certain things, like some of the stupid shit you say or with you smokin' ganj, I won't. 'Syour body, dude. Your temple." Brian wasn't looking around the room as he spoke, trying to put his eye on his image of Greta or in search of something more important he should have been doing. He was focused on this. "Do something stupid, though, like jammin' a needle in your arm or eatin' paper, or smackin' a girl around, and I'm afraid I'm gonna have to pull an intervention.

"You are my brother, Jay, and I'll always love you like one." He looked at me with a *do you understand?* look. And I did. I did understand.

"And someday when I have my 2.5 little Dildys with Guinevere, or whoever, I'll expect you to be godfather. I'll even call you Don. Unnastan', Pisan?" Brian rubbed my head using his best Corleone. "Got it?" Again, I did, and I gave my best friend a hug.

"Now, let's go get that chib a vodka Red Bull."

10. The Turning Point

It was 2:00 and I was still holding the same mixed-something, maybe a vodka Red Bull, I'd made over an hour ago, not wanting it at all but not putting it down. Surely that Murphy dude had written a law about it. "The second you put your vodka Red Bull down is the second you'll see the bowl of salty chips you'd been craving." I was still funny, in my mind.

It was our saying that if you can still feel your face you're not drunk enough, but I was saturated and tired and "drunk enough" to test that theory any more that evening.

Percentage-wise, score potential for arriving at a party after the bewitching hour is way low unless you already know the girl, or her crowd, or the girl/guy ratio is like 8:2. Otherwise, hang it up, because chances are good you'll just wind up getting in a scrap.

Unless your name is Brian Dildy, whose pheromones needed to be extracted for an infomercial or porn website product. They were true.

This evening, with his "smart-specs"---drug store fashion glasses that he joked about from the start as being just that, should the chib want to try them on to match prescriptions---and his wit, which was initiated by the smart-specs line, and the vodka Red Bull, he had his G.

What lessened the odds for Brian was that I had abandoned my wing man post and he was flying solo.

Greta's friend---one I'd seen several times prior, who knows where---whom I'd thought had lost weight, indeed had not, as a glance into a full length mirror of her posterior had revealed. Furthermore, she had a very loose, profane drunk tongue, saying "fuck" and "shit" a lot, and she smoked Marlboro Reds. Practically ate them. Not the image you'd expect of a girl named Hillary.

But Hillary had latched on to Jed, who never discriminated, and that was good for Brian, who had Greta's car keys and was making for the door, Greta slumped at his side like her bones had melted. "Gonna scope out Greta's dorm room, Jay. Says her roommate's gone for the weekend and she's gonna be all alone." Brian winked.

"Need a ride sweetie?" Greta asked. She was a very pretty girl, far as I could tell from the side of her that wasn't part of Brian. She had nice eyes, and unless it had come off throughout the evening, streak free, she wore little makeup. Natural. Brian did well.

I did well for Brian, and I was happy with that.

"Naw, guys, thanks. I'm outta the way. I'll just find Chat, and-"

"-dude, there's Chat," Brian nodded with his head towards the couch that had enveloped our horizontal friend, one leg bent upwards, one arm straight out with fingers splayed like a Christ figure, his mouth wide open to catch whatever anyone wanted to deposit. Someone had already balanced a styrofoam cup on his head.

"Well, shit," I said.

"Come on, Jay, it's cool."

"No, Bri, you guys go on. I'll just call Bill."

"Bill."

"Yeah, man. It'll at least show some responsibility on my part, ya know? Might even boost me a couple points for what's comin' with Markowski. Go on, I'll be fine."

"Sure?"

"Sure."

"Rightee-O, there, Don," Brian winked at me. "Rightee-O."

"Oh, and Brian?"

Brian looked at me. Greta was smiling. Natural. They actually looked like each other, a bit, like couples do who have been together a while.

"Call me tomorrow? That is, today. Shit, after my SAT classes. Call me later, though, okay?"

Brian smiled, and winked again. "I promise. You, my friend, will be the first I'll call."

CHAPTER TWO
SATURDAY

1. The Morning After

Note to self: Soju is bad. Soju is very, very bad.

Slats of dusty sunlight had been filtering through the blinds for some time. Days. The twittering birds were holding their weekend convention outside my open windows. The symposium had begun shortly after I'd gotten home and had faded in and out with consciousness.

There'd been no sleep. Only torpor.

The air was still, damp and thick, a magnified petri dish, yet my body was baked and cracked like a southwestern river basin. If I moved I would crumble. My tongue was primitive as it scraped across my lips of salted slugs, like slowly rubbing two full balloons together. My heart was now in my head and my brain had melted through my ears matting my hair to my scalp. I was mummified.

Add to this the trumpeting reveille of Bill, and you have a visual of Hell: Dante's *Inferno*, Milton's *Paradise Lost*.

Beth whispered *smile* to me as I shuffled to the bathroom. She winked. She knew. *Above everything,* she told me one time, *I act happy the morning after so he'll leave me alone.* Beth had many mornings after. She had it down.

They say it takes more muscles to frown than to smile. It took even more strength to fake it, so I did neither. I just spoke, as little as possible, and only when spoken to by Bill.

"Want some vitamins, Jay?"

"No, thank you."

"Here, these are what I take."

"Thank you."

"Have a glass of milk."

"I got a glass of orange juice. There's milk in my cereal."

"Want some cereal? Oh, you got some already. Good for you. Have some orange juice then."

"Already got it."

"Good for you." Pause. "Have part of the paper. Here."

"Thanks."

"Why do you like this cereal?" He looked at the box. I didn't answer, just kept eating, face in my bowl.

"Okay, then, you seem all set. I'll be in my study if you need me."

"Rightee-O."

"Beth said you can take her car to class this morning."

"Okay."

"There should be plenty of gas in it, but if you need to refill I go to the BP on Sunset, near the cleaners."

"Okay."

"Jay, are you listening?"

"YES." Audible sigh, couldn't help it. "Yes, Dad."

"And put the car in first gear if you park on a hill. It helps save the emergency brake."

"Got it. First gear."

"And remember that the lights on her car stay on a minute after you leave."

"Okay."

"Okay. Well, I'll be in my study if you need me. I said that already."

"You said that already."

I'd say he did it on purpose, to aggravate the hangover and thus acting as a deterrent for future excess. Only, this was every day, Bill's variation of "so, how's the weather?" I cannot recall ever having had a truly substantial conversation with the man, his mind always drifting to some far off place of unwashed dishes, bills or term papers, though there really ought to be an additional warning on any bottle of alcohol, particularly Soju, after the pregnant women and heavy machinery lines, **Caution: Bill may follow**.

2. News from Stu

SAT prep class was held in a tiered lecture hall at the local state college, and I, having arrived a mere five minutes late, was surprised to find almost all the seats occupied, especially the morning after the

Jeremy Stevens

biggest party of the year. I recognized a few faces as I quickly scanned the disgustingly bright-eyed, bushy-tailed lot, most of whom appeared to be present voluntarily, and I apologetically eased into the front row, catching the glare of the instructor and the wrinkled noses of those who were already sitting in the front row, voluntarily.

If there was a way to bottle and market everything about Jason Braswell that Saturday morning, alcohol-related incidences and attendance at 12-Step programs would surely plummet, making the world a happier, safer place for all. The scratch of my pen was as erratic as a needle on a polygraph, my heart a hollow rawhide drum keeping a tribal beat. The sweat, like this was *the* test; the vertigo, like I was claustrophobic on the top row; the smell, gaseous from my breath and liquid from my pores and solid from my being. I actually smelled myself.

I was slowly coming to. I much preferred the alternative.

"Braz, man, surprised to see *you* here." Stu was also a rising senior at Premier and was also at the party last night, though he was leaving when we arrived. Stu was All-Everything and was definitely eager about the classes, if not to better a score then for intellectual enrichment, though in sincere moderation he did like his beer and grass which made him a pretty cool cat.

"Stu, dude, 'sup brother." We clapped hands and bumped shoulders. "Bin needin' this break since my man began preachin'. Pepsi or somethin'?" I downed my soda. It was one of those pounds where you felt the coldness go all the way down. I bent to get another.

"Naw, I'm straight." He was looking at me funny, head tilted and mouth cornered upward like there was something he didn't get. "You okay, Jay?"

"No, Stu, I'm not. I feel like, like a piece of undercooked chicken, though thanks for asking. And how's yourself? How's the coxy?" I pounded my soda.

"Fine, Jay. I'm fine. Rowin's 'bout over." Still he stared, nonplussed.

"What?" I looked behind me on both sides, rubbed my nostrils, checked my zipper. "What?" I asked again between a laugh.

"You don't know, do you. You haven't heard."

"Heard what?"

Stu quickly looked around as if he needed help. He licked his lips, checked the corners of his mouth with his thumb and pointer. He evidently wasn't prepared for this.

"Heard what, Stu, dammit?" I made his eyes meet mine. My voice quickly became as carbonated as the second soda in my hand. Whatever this was, I wasn't prepared for it either. I thought I needed to sit.

"All's I know, Jay, is what I saw on the news this morning, that Dildy wrapped Greta Mackenzie's car around a tree driving her home from Brent's party." He spoke seriously, matter-of-factly, as if he'd been schooled on the scant details.

I did not blink. I did not breathe. I did sit, though. I finally sat, assuming the chair was still behind me. I just, sat.

"And. And what?" I looked up at Stu.

Stu slowly shook his head. "And what. Brian's out on bond and she's in a coma at regional." I planted my face in my palms. "Critical, Braz. Doesn't look too good, is my opinion."

3. A Curse

The dispatch for a single car accident on Safe Haven Road was overheard by paramedic Sergeant Andy Swanson, who was returning to Base from another incident in the immediate vicinity. Swanson knew precisely where the curve was, and for a long time in the back of his mind he had been waiting for this call.

Another Friday night, he sighed, and spit out his freshly packed wad of Copenhagen, thinking again that he needed to switch to long-cut for these shifts. A dip of long-cut he could save and reuse, an economical advantage during this thin time of diapers and formula.

"Medic eight, ten-seventeen," Swanson responded.

"Medic eight, ten-seventeen at 02:34. Ten-four."

Jeremy Stevens

The man at the curve with the blood soaked face looked more like a shocking phantasmagoric flash from a Wes Craven thriller. His arms looked broken, they were so limp by his side. His bent fingers cradled the cell phone.

The man was emotionless, perfectly still, a Halloween prop. He'd been to the beyond with sightless eyes.

Sergeant Andy Swanson pulled to the shoulder, grabbed his responder bag, and initiated routine procedure.

"Sir, are you hurt?" The man stared at Swanson. His pupils were dilated, a sign of brain injury, or of serious inebriety. The man smelled as though he'd been pickling for some time.

"Sir, are you hurt?" Swanson repeated, more slowly. The man might have been sleep walking. He had a thin, confused smile and was shaking his head ever so slightly as if saying *no, no, all wrong, do over* to this entire scene.

"Sir, I will need you to sit with me here so we can take a better look at you."

Swanson dabbed lightly at the man's face. "Sir, how many other people are in the vehicle?" The man still did not answer. *Bring it home, Swanson.* "Sir, what is your name?"

The man lifted his hand and looked at the phone like a marionette commanded by strings. He looked up at the paramedic, kneeling before him. Something did register. "Brian," the mottled-faced man answered. "Brian Dildy."

Sergeant Swanson discovered that a fairly deep gash in the forehead, one that would require stitching, and a steady nose bleed were the only sources of flow. His respirations appeared within normal limits. Swanson looked at the crumpled mass in the trees about twenty-five yards away. Unbelievable. Unless this man had some internal injuries, which was quite possible, he was absolutely a product of divine intervention.

"Thank you, Brian, very good. That's excellent. Brian, how many other people were in the vehicle with you?"

"One. Only one other, officer. Her car." Brian began mashing buttons. "Gotta call Jay. I promised I'd call him, first thing."

Sergeant Andy Swanson gently took the phone. "Time for that in a bit. Brian, the girl in the car. What is her name?" All responders were now arriving, EMS followed by fire and law enforcement. It was suddenly very loud, and colorful like a disco dance hall. "Billy, we gotta green tag here. One other's in the vehicle, condition unknown," Swanson called to a fellow EMT. The man nodded and foot-raced his partners.

"Sir?" Brian asked.

"What's the girl's name, Brian?" If Swanson could get a name, he could personalize his speech. Knowing the name always helped calm the victim.

"Greta," Brian answered. Swanson stared for a moment at the man sitting slouched, Indian-style in front of him, then flew off towards the woods as if from a starting line, leaving his responder bag open on the pebbly shoulder.

02:36 a.m.

Save the deployment of the airbag and the obvious smashed glass the driver's side appeared relatively accommodating, though there was the slightly torn seatbelt which told volumes about the driver's condition. Having struck the solid tree slightly right of center, however, the passenger's side was a mess, a polymeric labyrinth of metal, plastic, nylon, rubber and cracked solid glass containing a single static form.

Here also, amidst the gaseous vapors from the car's bowels, lingered the pungent odor of alcohol, a hopeful sign of life. Greta.

There was a fissure in the structure through which Swanson was able to affix a C-collar to immobilize the girl's neck. (Swanson thought "bobblehead," and dismissed it just as quickly.) He performed a quick trauma assessment: the right pupil was larger than the left, there was no reaction to light stimulus, and the blood pressure showed borderline hypertension. These were all signs of brain injury.

Greta. The child needed to be removed. Time was absolutely critical, considering her present condition and the volatile state of the automobile. The pneumatic wheezing of the Jaws of Life was audio to the horror show, creation of the folk tale of the "beast of the woods" for the Webelos Scouts camping miles away to tell their own children one day. The car moaned as it was gutted. The body was extracted ---*watch the fucking neck*--- and spider-strapped on a backboard for further immobilization.

Her face. Several teeth were missing and her tongue was halved. Her forehead and cheeks were lodged and bloodied with tiny fragments of automobile. Bones were protruding. Clear fluid was seeping from her nose and ears. Shit. "Billy, need a litmus on this."

Essentially, evidence of cerebrospinal fluid meant that the covering of the brain and spinal cord had breached, had opened, leaving room for infection. Bad, bad stuff.

"Goddam this chick is fucked." Swanson swivelled. Larry.

The crew had already begun with the two large bore Ringer's IV's, and the oxygen rebreather was in place. The synchronicity of the team, a sign of true experience. It was beautiful. "Billy, consider porting two milligrams Narcan, and don't forget blood sugar." Billy knew. "Larry, over here," and Larry the Cherry followed.

03:02 a.m.

It was on one of his debut runs ten years ago that Swanson had commented over the dying. The motorcyclist was as contorted as a boy's well-used action figure, his leather seared to his skin from the 200 meter skid. There was absolutely no way. The man was done.

Swanson's words may have been the last the man heard before he finally died two hours later; the man's guttural echo, *help me*, beneath his helmet still plagued the paramedic to this day.

"Larry, you're new. Listen carefully, 'cause there's no fucking time. The girl's name is Greta. She is alive, and she can hear you. Always fuckin' assume, Larry, until they've flatlined and the bag's been zipped, that they can hear every word you say. Is this clearly understood?"

"Yessir."

"And we're cool."

"Yes. Yes we are."

The patient had been prepped and was ready for transport. Sergeant Andy Swanson leaned closely and lightly swabbed around her nose. The CSF was at a slow trickle. *Come on, now, sweet Greta. Be strong for me.*

The ambulance sirened away. His cell began to ring, and his voice cracked as he answered.

"Hi honey, feeding time? No, nothing. Nothing's wrong, honey. Yes, I promise." He held the phone away to wipe the tears. This one had hit home, had penetrated his soul. This was the assignment he'd heard about. Sergeant Swanson had been initiated.

"Put my little girl on, would ya, hon?" He heard her breathing, her silly "baba, baba." He cried and smiled.

"Daddy loves you, baby," he managed. "Daddy loves his Greta."

4. The Markowski Exam

There would be no more SAT prep class that day as I promptly used word of my best friend's plight, instead of the pain of hangover, as a personal excuse to bail out early. The story saved my reputation, in my own mind; after all, you only "got game," have the fortitude to "hang," if you are able to responsibly face whatever the morning after brings. That includes SAT prep classes. "You drank the wine, you do the time," that sort of thing. That was the truest test.

The test.

To say that the Markowski test hadn't already crossed my mind would be a lie, because I needed that test to pass a final exam on Monday, in two days, which until present had consumed my own life. Acing that test. Erasing that 38.

And Brian had that test. And therefore, I needed Brian. Right?

I started Beth's car. I turned it off. Where am I going? *What the hell am I thinking?*

When I was young---Bill and Carol had been a couple of years into their divorce, but Bill hadn't met Beth yet---I had let Jason Porter ride my new Redline BMX bike, the kind which I told all the kids at school had "mag wheels" because I thought it should. He zipped across the street from between two parked cars just like Mom had told me repeatedly not to do, because I might get hit; and he got hit, and I heard the hit and saw a single shoe fly into the air.

The ambulance came, and the fire truck, and I saw them from a neighbor's porch where I sat crying; and the old lady who lived down the street, the one who always let her dog shit on our lawn, asked if I were the Jason they were taking to the hospital.

"Are you the Jason who got hit?"

"No. I'm the Jason whose bike got hit."

My friend was to spend a week in the hospital with a serious concussion, three broken ribs, a broken arm and a broken ankle. My bike, though, was pronounced DOA. That was *my* concern, back when I was young.

So. The sociology test eight hours ago wasn't of such paramount importance because, well, I was very drunk, but also because I assumed I'd be seeing Brian again today, to hint at it or request it outright. Best friends can do that, you know. Especially best guy friends. Girls get funny about that stuff.

Besides, he's the one who volunteered it in the first place.

But now. Shit. I'm fucked either way. If I don't request the exam, I fail sociology. If I do, I'm an asshole. I just need to hope that Brian remembers his offer, though come on now. Really. I may be his best friend, but I'm certain he's already called several other people this morning, despite his parting promise eight hours ago. Best friends can break promises, after all.

But these are all sick thoughts, anyhow, because it's not about me, right? Right. It's about a man who's probably very alone and scared and who's also completely fucked either way, and it's about a girl who no longer knows she's alive.

And these are all thoughts I need to bottle, thoughts I wouldn't dare tell anyone, even my best friend.

5. Bill's Take

I went by Brian's apartment but from what I could tell he'd never been home. Roz was still where we parked her. The blinds were still drawn.

There was a half-full bottle of beer next to the empty bottle of Soju on the balcony railing; cigarette butts and ash dusted the porch, and blackened cigarette marks were burned into the wood, for Chat smoked cigarettes when he drank.

I felt there should have been police tape cordoning off the area, like this was a crime scene. The entire complex felt vacant. I called his phone from my cell and heard it ringing from outside the door. I got his voice mail in his best Ben Stein, *These words are lovely, dark and deep, but I've got promises to keep, and miles to go before I sleep. So leave your message at the beep.* I didn't bother. I tried his cell, but it went straight to mail. Brian was definitely not home.

I tossed the party debris in the trash on the way to Beth's car and tried Jed and Chat, though it was still only 10:45. No such luck. Assuming Stu had his facts straight, which was a pretty safe assumption, Brian was probably at his parents' house, and their number wasn't listed; so, my only option now was to go home, to hope Bill was at the office because there would be questions. Lots and lots of questions, beginning with *why aren't you in class?* and ending with *and who's Brian again?* I wanted to search the net to find the news story from that morning for myself, as the Daily Rag hadn't printed it yet, and I wanted some quiet time to digest and plan the next step.

"Jason?" His chair pushed back in his study above and his moccasined footsteps purposefully strode to the foot of the stairs. Fuck. I felt like I'd

Jeremy Stevens

been caught at something. I didn't know whether to go up the stairs to meet him, or to have him come to me, though he didn't give me much time to think about it.

"Jason? Oh, huh, it is you. Did class let out early?"

"No, Dad. No. I heard some really horrible news about Brian, and I wanted to come home to see if I could find out more." It was all the truth, and the news indeed was horrible, yet I felt like I was acting it out, like I was improvising, like I was lying. I couldn't look at the man.

"So you left class early."

"I did. At the break."

(sigh) "Jason, at *which* break. They break three times." The man was paying for the sessions. He'd done his research.

"The first."

"Jason, damn. You simply cannot stay out until 2:30, drinking, the night before these classes. I'm on a fixed budget this month and wawahwawahwah..." His drone was like the canned voice on the other end of the Charlie Brown cartoon phone. Good grief. "....wawahwah cannot afford to have you leaving early."

"Dad, did you even hear what I said?"

(sigh) "About what, Jason."

"About Brian, God dammit. I need to find out if what I heard was true."

"I will not have you using that language around me, Jason Braswell. Now, think. Would the truth of whatever it is you're talking about be any different had you stayed for the entire session? Jason?"

In all appearances and actions I had suddenly become the poster child of America's defiant youth: arms tightly crossed, weight on one hip, opposite foot tapping, mouth closed in a frown; occasional sucking of the teeth, nostrils flared, very audible sighs, eyes fixed on one corner of the room.

I was the child you wanted to slap. *Listen, you little bastard.*

This is not what I had intended. I should have gone to the library to look the shit up.

"You knew you'd be leaving early when you drove off this morning, still smelling like a brewery."

"Okay, Dad, *enough*." I cut the air with my spread hand. I'd had enough. "Enough. My best friend Brian may be in a lot of trouble, so I'm just going to have to go ahead and excuse myself from this little chat we're having here, okay? Though I do so enjoy our catch-up time together." Father's tirade deserved a volley of sarcasm, my best line of defense.

"Best friend, who?"

"Brian."

"Okay, Jason. Okay." He paused. He tightened his eyes and squeezed the bridge of his nose, as if fighting off a migraine. He then lifted his leg a bit and cupped his other hand between his cheeks to silence the sound of a fart, and made the squinched face of one who is squeezing out a fart, and sighed as it escaped, soundless.

The man had it down. The silent fart.

One who didn't know Bill better might think this was his crass way of making light of a situation he didn't deem important. That interpretation certainly worked, present situation included, though I just chalked it up to another Billism, one of a great, great many.

"Better?" I asked. He didn't respond. He was already on to the next thing, what you'd call a sequential thinker.

"Brian. Okay. Now, you need to help me here, Jason. Which one's Brian?"

"You know, Huey, Dewey, Louie," I recited, sounding bored and really, really pissed.

"Oh," Dad chuckled. "One of *those* three."

6. Confirmation

"I'm standing at the Hawke Creek side of the curve on Safe Haven Road, about a quarter mile south of US 1, a curve apparently grossly misjudged at approximately 2:30 this morning by the driver of what remains of the vehicle you see behind me. Brian Christopher Dildy, twenty, of Meadowmont, was that driver, and has already been taken to Flint Regional for medical examination and observation. EMS crews have extracted the only passenger, Greta Ann Mackenzie, using the Jaws of Life. Ms. Mackenzie was not wearing her seatbelt, and has been described by EMS as 'unresponsive.' Alcohol *is* believed to be a contributing factor in this incident. Reporting from Safe Haven Road, which evidently has not lived up to its name this evening, I am Katie Christendon."

"Thanks, Katie. It has since been reported that bond was posted for Brian Dildy's release from the Flint County magistrate's office later this morning, and that he is facing the charges of DWI, reckless driving, and driving while having consumed alcohol under the age of twenty-one. Greta Mackenzie has been deemed comatose. We at the station will keep her in our prayers."

(side) "Poor girl."

(side) "Mmmmm. Tragic."

"In other news this morning...."

What remained of Greta's car looked as though it had been parked on top of a Miracle Gro bamboo seed: an enormous, possessed stalk with red demonic eyes and smoke jetting from its ears appeared to have sprouted through the vehicle's center. The night was sludge, and the camera and hospital crews had set up their tripod halogens which provided ample albeit milky light to show that there was no identifiable car. There did not even appear to be any salvageable parts.

The image, and the fact that Brian actually walked away from that thing, were true testaments to the importance of seatbelts.

Odds of Brian eventually getting a DWI were fantastic considering how often he drove drunk, or while drinking, or most often both.

But this. This I could not believe. Usually a man who crashes has priors, a history of alcoholism, a prison record. Something. It doesn't *just* happen. You have to build up to it: rising action to climax, three strikes you're out, the calm before the storm. Something. But this.

Brian put a girl in the hospital. Comatose. There were now so many variables for her: life, vegetable, death, and varying degrees of each. *Miles to go before I sleep.*

Life, vegetable, death.

Rock, paper, scissors.

Shoot.

I called Brian's parents' house but no one was answering. I didn't figure they would. . They lived according to "if it's that important they'll call back," and I did, repeatedly. One time it was busy, but when I called again a half minute later it rang which indicated others were trying to call too. I tried Jed and Chat again but they were hopeless.

I was fresh out of ideas and clueless what to do next. I paced around the den. I watched the video twice more. I viewed the local radio station's Babe of the Day. I checked my Yahoo account again. I sharpened some pencils. I scrolled the missed calls list on my phone. I viewed the babe, again.

And then Beth came home.

7. Beth and Bill

She'd made a quick trip to the mall to exchange an outfit and her life-long friend drove, leaving me her car for the SAT prep class. Beth too was surprised to see me home; however, had she been the one to meet me at the door, instead of Bill, I might have been in a better place mentally. Beth was the perfect antithesis of her husband. Their marriage was an anomaly.

"Jason, what's happened?" were her very first words as she came into the den to find me staring at the computer screen, back to the news center's site. "What's wrong?" I knew she hadn't talked to Bill because he was now in the backyard, watering his garden. I could see him from where I sat. She just sensed something was wrong.

"Afternoon, there, Beth," I said, not looking up. "What makes you think something's wrong?"

"Well, there, Jay," she began in imitation, "for starters, you're home. Usually when I loan you my car you take advantage of the situation."

"Check." She had a point. "Beth, you remember Brian, right?" I left the screen to face her, swiveling one-eighty in the chair. "Brian Dildy?"

"Sure I know Brian. Silver Bullet Brian. Cutie pie, that one."

"So it's not hard to keep my friends straight, then," I asked, again looking out at Dad, who was now cleaning up after the dog with the yellow rubber dish washing gloves he kept turned inside out in a pail in the garage. "Sure's difficult for some folks."

"Jay, you take the man too seriously. Your father is a different breed, is wired a bit differently. But he is a good man, and he does love you very much."

"You're too kind. Different breed. You know what they say about the apple and the tree, Beth."

"Okay, well, let's just say you haven't fallen yet. How's that?"

"Maybe I'll be blown off, just down the road a bit. A big ol' storm." Dad was now scratching his ass, lost on some weighty topic. "Anyhoo, about Brian, there, Beth. Gotta 'nother minute?"

"Uh-oh, okay now. A talk. Lemme fix a drink first," she said, looking at her watch. "Hold that thought. Back in a jiff."

"Fix me one too, will ya?" I said in obvious jest, with obvious levity, obviously to the computer screen which I was now once again facing to recall the video for Beth. I was waiting for the obvious reply of "ha ha."

"I take mine with a splash. Tell me if you think it's too much."

What'd she say?

The differences between Beth and Bill seemed to far outweigh the commonalities and not in areas that didn't matter.

Their marriage was as odd as that logic.

They were both "academic" extremes, Dad the professor and Beth the elementary school teacher; they had both been previously married, twice even; they both enjoyed the outdoors, theater, and finer dining.

And probably, alone as they did these things, they both enjoyed each other.

But at home there was stress, and very little laughter that wasn't contrived. I'm talking fidgeting, nail-biting-eyes-closed-head-shaking-cold-sweat, tense stress that made me never, ever want to have company over.

No wonder Dad had trouble with names. There were seldom faces to go with them.

Bottom line: Bill was a social embarrassment. If it didn't interest him, he was in his study; and if he caught the look in Beth's eye that said he needed to be there, he was thinking about his study.

When he wasn't spaced out, he was anxious.

If he ever became engaged, he needed punch lines repeated.

Where Bill pondered over why a person would call during a meal, Beth just answered the phone; where Bill complained about the dog having escaped, Beth got the dog; where the English muffin wasn't fork-split, Beth didn't comment; where the neighborhood boy didn't mow the lawn in horizontal rows, Beth didn't care.

If she forgot the bread she just went back to the store. Simple. If she'd never heard a slang expression, like "bling" or "dawg," that was acceptable. If the car in front of us used too much oil, well phooey on them.

With Bill, block off the next five to twenty minutes for commentary. It was the closest you'd come to a conversation.

However, bar none, the most baffling contrast in their marriage, the most eyebrow-raising, jaw-dropping aspect, was that Dad had been sober approximately five years, completely free from the substance that destroyed his relationship with his wife, my mother, and that made a some-time son of me, when he chose to marry a woman who was, unquestionably, alcoholic with her drinking.

Bill had been married twice prior. There was some phantom woman before Carol, my mother; and the only thing I know about her is that he met her in Africa. What her name was, or any physical description, or whether or not *she* drank, or even whether she was another white Peace Corps volunteer or a Yoruba tribeswoman left much to the imagination.

If raised, it was all just dismissed as "a lifetime ago."

However, Bill did not react well to blips in the radar, the reason I believe I chose to stay with him and Beth more than Mom. Any volatile situation, anything that jeopardized his equilibrium, was often readily dismissed. This loaned itself nicely to my social obligations, leaving school early and drinking scotch during midday and the like.

8. Beth's Advice

She sipped at her Dewar's with a splash like she'd be at it all day. Moderation is the key. I killed mine in ten minutes. If she noticed, she didn't comment.

"Has anyone called you?"

"Not on my cell, and nobody has the number here. Maybe Mom's, though I haven't checked."

"Jason, you need to go see him."

"Think so?"

"Yes I think so. If it were first thing in the morning I'd say wait, but it is 12:30 and I think enough time's passed. Brian needs to see a familiar face, I think. Especially yours. You can take my car. But Jason, please, by all means..."

"...I just don't want him to think I'm rubbernecking, like sponging off his misfortune, you know? People do that, prob'ly been calling him all morning. Makes 'em feel better about themselves."

"You're a good person, Jason, and you have a good heart. Now go. Be a best friend."

Beth and her scotch had lightened my mood and I left for Brian's parents' house ready to face his reality, hoping beyond hope that amidst all his grieving he remembered the Markowski test, had brought it with him from his own apartment because he had promised it to me, after all; and that he had it ready, voluntarily, so I could pour all my energy, my entire good heart, solely into him, undistractedly.

Although my own experience with alcohol was shallow, it was enough for me to have known better. I quickly scarfed down a rocks tumbler of scotch a bit after noon, to relieve a discomfort already induced by alcohol, when two ibuprofen and a lot of water, or sweet acidophilus to coat the stomach, would have been sufficient.

Brian, always chock full of really interesting stuff, called it hair of the dog, citing Scottish lore that if you put a few strands of hair from the rabid dog that bit you on the wound, it would help ward off evil spirits. Similarly, if you drink more alcohol to relieve a hangover, it will help reduce the pain.

And it did, temporarily, and as I drove to Brian's I thought it was going to be a gentle landing, a nice, calm reintroduction to mainstream society.

Maybe for other people, but for me?

Well, I just got really tired, and irritable, and I thus foresaw two options for the rest of this day: to suck it up and go to bed, admitting defeat, that I couldn't hang and that I'd see ya tomorrow, "you're right, there, Bill, drinking last night was a bad idea"; or, to drink more.

Moderately, of course, but more.

If I wanted to stay glued this afternoon for the job that needed to be done, I needed to drink more.

This is a grim scene, man. This is dark. We're talking David Lynch here, a little Joel and Ethan Coen perhaps. It is almost 1:00. Twenty minutes ago I finished a generous tumbler of scotch with my step-mother. I am now cradling a 40 oz. Bud between my legs. I am driving to visit my best friend who has just been released from jail for DWI, and a girl he knows nothing about lies on a gurney in the ICU.

He put her there. Comatose. She might die.

If she dies, he goes to prison. Prison, not jail. Prison. For a long time.

If she dies today, he is arrested today. If he is arrested today, I fail sociology.

Mrs. Tepas was my geometry teacher. She looked like Margaret Hamilton. She boasted quite often the fact that in thirty years she had only missed one day of school. We lamented this fact, quite often. *I'll get you, my pretties.*

Mrs. Tepas taught us proofs. Deductive reasoning.

If A=B, and B=C, **then** A=C
Axiom 1: If Greta dies (A), Brian goes to prison (B).
Axiom 2: If Brian goes to prison (B), I fail sociology (C).
Conclusion: If Greta dies, I fail sociology.

9. Trauma II

They were hurrying to wait for the red tag patient at Trauma II like restless families of passengers faced with flight delay, milling about and eyeing watches, pen-tapping clipboards, triple checking equipment and the security of connections. It was a reunion, of sorts, and everyone had made it: the ER staff and respiratory therapy; radiology and cardiology; the reporting nurse; and the trauma surgeon on duty, lead man Dr. Michael Pittman. They were all waiting at Trauma II, ready to swarm the hapless victim like army ants on carrion.

A morbid visual, Dr. Pittman agreed, but accurate nonetheless.

The rapidly approaching sirens -runners, take your mark- and one final courtesy transmission of their imminent arrival -get set- and it was on.

Go.

03:15 a.m.

The patient was delicately yet expeditiously moved to the ER stretcher where she was promptly stripped of all modesty. Her clothes were sheared off, from her sexy strapless top down to her shit-soaked panties; her personals were bagged and charted; and a Foley catheter was inserted, up past the stud pierced through her clitoris, to drain the urine.

There was no reaction to reflex stimuli, and her Glasgow scale of response (eyes, verbal, motor) was E2V2M1 at 3:17 a.m., where any total score < 8 indicated coma. However, her lungs were clear, her bowel sounds were good, and her urine was clear and plentiful from the alcohol.

What Dr. Pittman needed most urgently was a CT scan of the child's head and neck.

Meanwhile, what Charge Nurse Marissa Alvarez needed was information, and none was readily available.

County EMS had done a quality job, but with differing personalities and idiosyncrasies, "schools of thought," in the vast strata of the medical profession, nothing is ever perfect. Dr. Michael Pittman, for instance, would have IV'd the girl with 100 mg of thiamine, in addition to the narcotics reversal, because alcohol was present. *Minor oversight, though*, even the doctor was willing to concede.

But Nurse Alvarez, who was already a "fiesty little one," considered it "very, very unfortunate that the paramedēcs forgot the purse."

"Who is dēs child? I need to know. Her parents, they need to know, too!"

It wasn't enough that her name was Greta and that the cops were en route with "the damn purse," as one fed-up medic retorted.

Nurse Marēsa, she was funny like that.

03:27 a.m.

Radiology confirmed Dr. Pittman's fears. The CT scan and c-spine revealed acute frontal subdural hematoma with evidence of diffuse cerebral edema, or swelling, secondary to brain shear injury. Dr. Pittman knew these were indicators of impending transtentorial herniation.

Broken down, in language he would soon use in an inevitable conversation, if the swelling, and therefore the pressure, continued, the brain would have no place to go but down. A complete fall into the brainstem, an event as unpredictable as a jungle storm, would result in immediate respiratory arrest.

Main switch pulled. Total loss of power.

It was imperative now to address the swelling, and that required last resort procedures. Pittman's nurse was told by neurosurgery to prep a craniotomy tray with 2% Lidocaine, an antiseptic, for drilling. Mannitol was ordered to reverse the swelling, and due to urgency would be IV'd as a bolus versus a drip; while that was prepared by pharmacology, Solu-Medrol would be used as a stop-gap.

As Greta's condition had not become respiratory, Pittman did not want to intubate. Not yet. Removal of subdural blood from the head---a large section of skull would actually be cut out---and a rapid introduction of the reverse osmotic mannitol might be enough to stabilize the condition.

Of course, these were all first instincts. Dr. Michael Pittman did not have the luxury of time for mental debate. Really, he was in God's territory now, a very scary place if thought about too long. Dr. Michael Pittman was not God. Michael David Pittman was a man, a servant of God but a man nonetheless, able to make human mistakes.

Just not this morning.

So intubation would wait. He needed to have one last thing, but in due time.

Right now, the doctor needed a cold splash of water, a vigorous tooth brushing, and five minutes of quiet darkness, to regroup, to become whole.

Her name was Greta Ann Mackenzie. In her purse was found a single unopened condom, a lighter, a half-smoked marijuana cigarette, and a wallet containing everything you'd expect to find in a wallet including, quite fortunately, an emergency contact card. *Please, dear, for us, okay? You just can never be too careful.*

Robert and Margaret had received that night-shattering call they'd worried about since their only baby first packed for college. They were on their way from Braxton, a fifty-minute drive this morning cut in third, and Dr. Pittman was going to need to be what no medical school, anywhere, could teach.

He was going to need to be Michael.

10. Back When

Padded footsteps, a parted curtain, hushed voices and a lady, Brian's mother, said my name; the chain rattled and the deadbolt clicked and somewhere between the opening and closing of the heavy front door I stepped into the lonely grey foyer. It had institution-stillness, heavy with sentiments: of paths not traveled, of scenarios, what-ifs. It had the quietude of a narthex with a similar blossomy, antiseptic smell. The only sounds were the ticking of the clock, the hum of the air conditioning. The three looked wan, dusty, like they should have been wearing paper slippers and paper robes you put on backwards, especially Mrs. Dildy, who was always so sprightly.

We all hugged wordlessly, like we knew a bug had been planted and our conversation was being taped; we gave firm embraces with sincere burp-pats to the back. Brian's parents then went their own separate ways, one down the hazy corridor, one up the stairs, slowly and remorsefully like they were each in their own individual way to blame.

The scene was set for Rod Serling to step out from behind the staircase and begin his introduction, for this was not the residence I recalled from two years prior.

When Brian graduated from high school his parents threw a party with a string quartet and an ice sculpture of a raised hand holding a diploma. Waitresses in tuxedo tops with red bow ties and cummerbunds offered grilled shrimp and scallop skewers, cantaloupe and prosciutto, spanakopita, and mini brie and bacon quiches; out back, Brian's father and a neighbor tended to the clam bake while his mother served the spirits. (With prior parent approval of course, and with carefully monitored restrictions.) It was a delicate affair, where the girls behaved like debs and the guys, their dates.

Gabrielle and Brian fed each other strawberries dipped in the chocolate fondue fountain, not in a gross just-got-married fashion but quite elegantly on lawn chairs beneath the flowering magnolia. As I was the only underclassman I sort of just helped here and there, drifting between groups and collecting abandoned strong-plastic picnicware, flirting with the pretty waitresses. I actually got a number but she never called back because I lied and told her I had graduated too.

Brian's mom Catherine had a very pretty smile and dazzling teeth and she looked about ten years younger with her hair back in a pink bow, and his father was really cool to be around, wearing Asics without socks and cargo shorts. He was interesting and interested, the kind of dad who remembers your friends' names, and he and his wife touched each other playfully and he patted her on the tush, and their happiness was infectious. With Catherine and Christopher, it was no wonder Brian was such a neat guy.

But today, there were no balloons. There was no music, no fresh summer breeze through the window screen, no verdancy. There was no laughter, no raised toasts to brand new beginnings.

Today there was the hellish uncertainty of an abrupt end.

Today, there was prayer.

11. The River

"This cool?"

"'Course, Jay, you're straight. Need you to get me outta here, though, for an hour or so. That cool?"

"Cool. I got Beth's car for the afternoon." I gave Brian a quick once-over. "Man, I gotta tell ya. You look really fuckin' good for what you came out of."

"'Bout ten stitches in the melon and a half-dozen cracked ribs from the seatbelt, or the airbag. Both maybe."

"Unbelievable. You oughta be thankin' somebody."

"Maybe. Make it to your classes this morning?"

"Yea, but in body alone and only part of the morning at that. Couldn't hang."

"Shit takes practice, Jay. Like learning a whole new culture."

We headed down the brick steps. It was a glorious early June afternoon in temperature, color, and smell: time-capsule glorious, like when another one comes along that matches you instantly recall where you were, what you were doing, and who you were with "on this day in that year."

But today. Today needed cloudy and overcast, cold and damp, spray-bottle mist for that static frizz. No amount of sunlight could lift the spirit. The good things were wasted today.

"Listen, I know this is gonna sound really whacked, but what say we get a six and go down to the river." It was a question Brian had to build himself up to ask.

I was glad he did. I just now needed the courage to ask mine.

"Done. I actually shared a cocktail with Beth not too long ago, talkin' 'bout 'really whacked.'" I didn't feel it necessary to tell him about the forty.

"Hair of the dog. Thought I smelled it, thought 'that's too fresh to be mornin' after.'"

"No way."

"Way. Really, dude. That mint you were suckin' on didn't do shit."

"Confirms somethin' right there."

"What's that?"

"That was an Arby's after-dinner from the Cruz pull. Had one left over in my pocket this morning."

We sat on the bank in the latticed shadows of the willows, tossing in twigs to race the current and coarse stones to smooth over time, calmed by the mesmeric babble. Forest birds poked around for home improvement, or lunch, rustling through the fragile dried and curled leaves matting the floor of the brambled undergrowth. Squirrels played tag. Moths jerked about, like bait. The mosquitoes hummed in and out like a plucked tuning fork.

And Brian cried. Without sniffles or whimpers or Kleenex, the water just fell unregulated from two dark, dead holes. We threw stones and raced twigs and drank beer without a goal because we both had promises to keep; in moderation, because today our togetherness had a certain, finite conclusion.

All that was real, inevitable, awaited, like the lonely Sunday blues.

"I am so sorry," he said to the river. I thought to reply, but I remembered Beth's advice, to just listen. That was best now. That was certainly easiest.

"I am so, so sorry." Brian faced me. Drips fell from his chin as if from a pointed beard. "No point in that now, huh?" I faced him back. My lips pressed lightly and pushed in at the corners, my eyebrows raised in that *I have so much to say, I have absolutely nothing to say* expression. "Yeah, not much point." His own lips vibrated air in a heavy sigh as he threw a stone at a chipmunk. Wide right.

"I fucked up, Jay. Plain and simple. I fucked up. My parents' lawyer came over this morning and he and I had a little heart to heart, straight talk, 'just the facts, ma'am.' He wanted to know everything, from how much I drank last night to how much I drank on a regular basis to who I drink with, to how often I drank and drove, and who I most often drank and drove with, and what I drank and where I usually bought it, and when, and yadayadayada. Spit-fire questions, Jay. No levity, like any one particular answer would warrant a 'well, 'least we got that in your favor'-type response. And 'onlys' didn't fly with ol' Stan, like when I hopefully said, 'I only drank on weekends,' like that was better news. Might as well have said I had the shakes so bad I drank my own piss when the liquor stores had closed.

"Dude didn't smile at all. When I was done giving him my drunk-a-logue he closed his notebook and just bullied right into the grim facts, no deposit in the emotional bank account like 'we're gonna get you outta this, Brian,' but beginning with, 'Brian, you need to listen very, *very* carefully to what I have to say,' only I knew it was only going to be bad, no 'blessing or curse' shit like with Cruz."

Brian finished his beer and opened his second and finally wiped his face with his sleeve, and finally sucked up his snot. The tears seemed to have stopped for the moment. I too finished my beer and got up to pee.

I thought it was going pretty well, all things considered. I was being a good listener, though I was stuck a bit on the "who with" question, wondering if Brian had given his lawyer my full name.

The Markowski test, and now this.

The loads we carry.

"I've thought about it a lot over the past, what time is it?" I checked my watchless wrist and shrugged my shoulders. "Well, over the past however many hours, and what it all boils down to is this." He looked at me to make sure I was paying attention. I looked like I was. "With every decision we make in our lives, we stand at a turning point. We are thrown some options, and we choose. Freewill. I'll take what's behind door number three. *The Lady, or the Tiger*. 'Member that story?" I nodded yes. "So we choose. Sometimes we aren't given much time, like Dale Jarrett---think that's his name---has to make, like, thousands of split-second cup-or-no-cup, life-or-death decisions in the course of one race. That example mighta sucked, but you get the picture." He still had me. "But oftentimes we have a chance to deliberate with the ol' conscience there, and that's where things can get really fucked up.

"See, Jarrett can walk away from that race, unscathed and accident free and with the money and the girl because he didn't have time to think. He always went with his first instincts, just like we were taught to take tests. 'Shit, I had C the first time.' Ya know?" I nodded. "But allow some wiggle room for 'perhaps maybes,' which almost always equates with greed or what's good for your own damn self, and you got a real fuckin' mess."

"Especially if you've been drinking," I offered.

"Oh, always if you've been drinkin', Jason, but not only." Brian took a long drink. I did too. We finished our second together.

"So, then, in a way Jed was right."

"Huh?" Brian responded, as if such a notion were preposterous.

"Jed, last night, when he was talkin' 'bout you not lying to the cop, and what a guy's natural inclination would be to do."

"Which is?" He was really trying to figure this one out.

"To lie to the cop. You don't remember, do you?"

"Sketchy. Any other key words?"

"Um, yea. John Bunnell."

"There it is, I remember now. Yea, Jayman, guessin' Jed *was* right, the rascal."

I had to remind myself that the pontificating and comfortable numbness were not preludes to something greater that evening, though Brian was beginning to sound now almost as if there were no issues.

And maybe, in the grand scheme of things, there really weren't. Maybe this really was one of those "we'll look back on it all and laugh"-life lessons, and that his lawyer was simply doing his job. I casually popped my third and handed Brian the opener and his last beer. Brian set them aside and continued so as not to lose his focus.

"I mean, sometimes it's just random chance, like, like those passengers on *Airplane!*---you saw the movie *Airplane!*---who had a choice between chicken or fish, and those who chose fish got violently ill."

"Right. Leslie Nielson had the lasagna." Here we go. This was good.

"Somethin' like that. Right. But those people didn't think, probably, 'shit, if I choose fish I'm gonna go into convulsions.' They just fuckin' chose fish." Brian fumbled with the opener but couldn't make it fit. He was shaking, and this time and incredibly suddenly the tears were accompanied by all that was "crying," the snotty snorts and the spasmodic attempts to keep speaking, and the coughs from shortness of breath and some clenched-teeth anger, brief wheezes sounding like a car that would just not turn over.

"And then." He coughed loudly and spat-up some beer and bile and the last of it hung pathetically in a sinewy strand from his chin, and he did not attempt to wipe it away but instead he doubled over, cradling his stomach in an apneic fit.

Not only did I just listen. I just sat there. Beth hadn't briefed me on this one. I just sat there, watching my friend collapse.

"And then you got Cruz," he managed after a few more dry heaves, sitting up and carelessly, unapologetically wiping his acidic spittle and gossamer gluey spill from his mouth and the front with his coat. "Brother did me a good turn, and while at the time I had dropped a huge load I didn't learn shit-all from it. I played the hand I was dealt, and I lost. I played the fucking hand at that turning point because I wanted to bed that girl instead of going with my gut instinct and folding, calling it a night and crashing on a couch like Chat. And now, NOW," Brian yelled, disturbing absolutely nothing, "a good man is going to lose his job in the public eye and-"

"-you're taking this a bit far, Brian. No one has to know about the pull except you and me, and I ain't tellin' shit."

"That, my friend, is where you're wrong, on two accounts," Brian said with a titter that brought me to full attention. If there were background music, it would have stopped abruptly at this crescendo.

"What?"

"Jay, I had to tell Stan everything---Stan's the lawyer---and that included the earlier stop. 'Sides that, Jed and Chat know too, remember? Word's probably spread all the way to the beach by now from all the weekend mall traffic."

"You talk to them since?"

"Chat called at about 10:30 and left a pissed message about 'leavin' a nigga' and 'some muthafuckin' friends I got.' Obviously hadn't heard yet about the crash. 'Least I hope not, from his tone."

"Neither's called since?"

"My phone's been off. But Jay, listen, man, there's this second thing about 'you not tellin' shit.'"

"I won't, Bri. Promise. Lips are sealed, 'bout Cruz and whatever else-"

"-Jay, shut the fuck up and listen, please? You are gonna be involved in this thing, Jay. They're gonna call you and visit you and pull you from class and all that after-school special shit. They're gonna turn the back of the chair around to face you and they're gonna straddle the seat and ask if you smoke or if you want a Coke. And then, Jay, they're gonna tear into you as if you were the one put that girl in the ICU."

"Why? I mean, why? What for?"

"Because you and I are best friends and the world knows we run together. And if that little girl dies, Jason, the prosecution is going to need you."

"To say what? To say that we drank beer together?"

"To say every goddamned thing the judge needs to hear to prove that this was not an isolated incident."

"YOU'VE NEVER FUCKING CRASHED BEFORE!" We were now standing and our faces were within a foot of each other and we were poking each other's breast bones to prove points. "This *is* isolated, Brian!"

"NO! I've driven drunk before. You know it. Jed and Chat know it. Officer Cruz, he knows it too."

"I'll lie, Brian. I'll lie, and-"

"-listen, you little bastard," and he grabbed me and hugged me and now I was crying too. I hugged him back and I cried, sobbed, as if I were the one who put the girl in the ICU. "Listen," he pushed me away to face me. Whatever tears he had left were serpentining across his graphite-stained cheeks. "You'll be subpoenaed. You lie, you'll perjure yourself. Jason, fuck. Just keep it simple, alright? Just tell what you know."

"But why do they need me?"

Brian sighed, stuttered-air like one who's had a very emotional last hour. "If she dies, Jay, they'll need you to determine what happens to me."

12. First Impressions

They both wore ball caps of their respective alma maters, rival basketball universities that saw game day at the center of the only family rift. They both wore jeans and running shoes. They both wore matching Brinkley sweatshirts.

Far too warm for heavy sweatshirts, but their outfits were not planned. They just grabbed and ran.

Robert and Margaret sat side by side, very closely, arms entwined and both hands held like newlyweds, their faces a dry montage of every expected emotion. Michael Pittman made the introductions---himself, Marissa Alvarez, and Hospital Chaplain Dennis Honeycutt---and the Mackenzies dispensed with the niceties of standing and handshaking, simply nodding in acknowledgment.

Though they both tarried a bit longer on the third.

"Why's he here?" Mrs. Mackenzie angrily demanded with pointed finger, as if the two shared some sordid past.

"Honey-"

"-don't 'honey' me, Bob, dammit." She threw his hands aside. "Doctor, what in the hell is going on here?"

And this was where experience was helpful, because natural inclination had once told the doctor to pacify them with advice on their breathing methods and anxiety control. *Now, I'm going to need for you to settle down, to take a few deep breaths for me*, that sort of thing.

Patronize them, like scolded children. Prolong the torture by making them obey first.

Nope, not today.

Pittman needed to time his compassionate pauses, select the correct voice, give the parents what they needed to know and answer their questions carefully, all with direct, confident eye contact. Generally, after it was presented, they ran the show.

"Approximately ninety minutes ago, Greta was involved in a very serious car crash. She was not wearing her seatbelt." Margaret's hand clasped over her mouth; Bob shifted, breathed deeply through his nose.

"Injury to her head has caused significant internal swelling, and surgery will be performed immediately to attempt to release the pressure."

"Is my baby still breathing?" Margaret asked immediately.

"She is breathing, and independently at that, but," the doctor raised his hand to her sign of relief, so as not to lead them astray, "but, Mr. and Mrs. Mackenzie, she is comatose, and if the condition worsens we will have to intubate."

"Doctor, I don't know what that means-"

"-it means they're gonna stick a tube down her. Doctor, was she drinking?"

"Robert-"

"-yes sir, she was," Dr. Pittman answered, and here once again he found himself at a crossroads. Easy it would have been to say that the driver had been too, but they didn't know anything about the boy.

Driver. Boy. Imagine the reaction. No. Leave that mess for law enforcement.

This was about effect, providing sketchy cause. This was about Greta Ann. Focus on her.

"God DAMMIT. How many damn times have I told her-"

"-Mēster Mackenzie, please. The drēnking, it is not important," Marissa Alvarez calmly interjected.

"Doctor Pittman to Trauma Two stat, Trauma Two stat." The PA boom in the small family room startled everyone, like a command from Big Brother.

"Nurse, do you have this?"

"Yes. Go now, Michael."

Charge Nurse Marissa Alvarez would do fine, very well in fact, for her talents lay in human relations, especially with the aggrieved parent. Nurse Alvarez was never able to bear children of her own, but instead of harboring a resentment she dedicated her life to helping those who could.

"Sadder it is to watch it die than never to have known it," she attempted once, many years ago, in explanation to Dr. Pittman over coffee. "Do you understand, Michael?" He did, and to this day those words have seen him through some very difficult, personal trials expressing sympathy.

"Doctor, she's stopped breathing. We already intubated at the direction of-"

"-did you check ABG?"

"O2, CO2, pH, they all check out."

"I need a CT scan of the head, stat," though Pittman knew. He knew. Balanced arterial blood gases indicated that up until a dramatic point, the body's respiratory system had been stable, without any gradual, undetected deterioration. That dramatic point, as the scan showed, was brainstem herniation.

Lights out. Total loss of power.

"Diane?"

"Yes, doctor."

Shit. "I'm gonna need you to cancel neurology. Please, get someone to help you prep this child for visitation in ICU, and let me know when she's ready, alright?" The blood and CSF and various sputa and leakage had been hastily smeared away for convenience and as an anti-contamination precaution, but nothing had yet been done cosmetically.

"Right away."

"And Diane, listen." Pittman caressed Greta's hand. "I know you know this, but hear me out anyhow. Please, bear in mind that even though she's on a machine, she's still very much alive in the eyes of many." He took off his wire-rimmed glasses, wiped them on his coat, and massaged the bridge of his nose.

"Of course."

"And if you talk, talk lovingly. Assume she can hear you, okay? Because this child," Pittman now whispered, looking at Greta's closed, dead eyes, "she's still somebody's baby."

13. Officer Cruz

To everyone who knew him, William "Monty" Cruz III was a good man. When Trooper Mitch Birnbaum had his deviated septum operation, Monty visited the hospital with cheeseburgers and beer; when Rose's, in the clerk's office, canary died, Cruz sent a card; and when Bailiff Dudley's granddaughter was recognized by the mayor for above and beyond service, it was Officer William Cruz who voluntarily represented the department at the ceremony and the reception. Cruz was everything fair and impartial, who "always did unto others as if he were the others." He was the go-to guy for personal problems, a confidant to many, a model of altruism.

His family likened him directly to his grandfather, a highly decorated World War II hero whose draft into the military saved him from an otherwise certain, dim future at Sing Sing. The neighborhood had dubbed him incorrigible, a juvenile delinquent, a misfit youth. The United States Armed Forces made him grow up.

William Cruz loved his grandfather, very much, and was proud to be his namesake. William Cruz Sr., who died the year his grandson was inducted into the Force, demonstrated the truest rags to riches rise of the human condition, and had instilled in his grandson, among other invaluable traits, the importance of forgiveness.

It was because of Officer William Cruz's reputation that Sergeant James Cleary was not at all surprised by the candor he displayed Saturday morning. He would have expected nothing less. William Cruz had always been a straight shooter, a genuinely good man, and Sergeant Cleary was proud to have him on his team.

"Good morning, Sarge. Gotta minute?"

"Gotta minute in a minute, William. Why don't you have a seat, shut the door behind you if you feel." Officer Cruz did just that as Cleary once-overed his document Before pressing *send*. "Thinking about e-mail I hate," he said as a filler, "is sending it, then spending the day wondering who you pissed off." Cruz did not respond, knew he didn't need to, but instead just casually surveyed the broad assortment of framed diplomas, certificates, and family photos: his knock-out wife, Lisa; his cheerleader daughter, his All-Conference son. All blonde, blue eyes. Beautiful family. Lucky, lucky man.

"And-that-should-do it," Cleary concluded with one final, harder tap of a button, presumably *send*. "Okay, what's the word?" Sergeant James Cleary gave Cruz his full attention.

"Sarge, I made a decision yesterday that will raise some questions, and I wanted to be the first to tell you so you didn't get blindsided." Cleary folded his hands on the desk, a silent prompt to continue. *Go on. I'm all ears.*

Cruz gave him the details, leaving nothing out.

Cruz: Car 211, 10-61. (traffic stop)
Communications: Go ahead Car 211.
Cruz: 10-61 at Clarendon and Charleston with Adam, Tom, Tom-1911, red, four-door Ford Taurus, occupied two-times. (location, license plate number, description)
Communications: 10-4, Car 211.

Dildy, Brian Christopher. Twenty years of age. License number 10012807. Speeding, 75/55 two years ago. No other priors. Pulled for a broken taillight. Odor of alcohol on driver's breath. Uncle is Pete Dildy, auto mechanic at Ingold's. Has saved me a fortune. Good man. What to do here? Monitor driver's response to questioning.

Mr. Dildy, had anything to drink this afternoon?
Yes. Yessir, I have.
Decision time.
I am going to follow you back to.......

Cruz: Car 211.
Communications: Go ahead 211.

Cruz: 10-24, Code-10, 10-8. (completed assignment, no action by officer, back in service for calls)

Communications: 10-4, 211.

Cruz spilled it all in necessary detail, and for about twenty seconds Sergeant James Cleary sat silently, hands in prayer fashion, lightly tapping his lips in thought and appraising not the scenario nor the man's abilities, but jumping ahead to the possible outcomes.

Absolutely there were mistakes made, as Cruz himself identified in his summary: he had permitted an impaired, underage man to drive when, if the decision was to release him, he should have made him walk, or driven the man himself. Cruz would be disciplined for this. However, Officer William Cruz was also a pillar of excellence in law enforcement, already corporal material after only about five years. This would not be overlooked.

No. This was not about Police Officer Cruz. This was about William Cruz III, the man right there in the chair. The prick editor of the Times, however, would jerk off with this new feed, and would use an individual person as an attempt to disgrace an entire department, taking flagrant liberties with the unspoken fine-line between the law and morality.

This was going to wind up a test of one man's fortitude, and knowing Cruz and his faith in the goodness of humanity, the next month, at least, was definitely not going to be easy.

"Alright, let's put aside for the moment the obvious strikes for conduct unbecoming. There were some violations of protocol, you've recognized them; procedure now as you know is for me to turn it over to Captain Vincent, who will in turn take it to IA for investigation."

"How do you think they'll take it, Sarge?" Cruz was on the edge of his seat, sitting upright like a first-timer in the principal's office. "I mean, with your experience and all."

"William, I'm flattered, but my experience doesn't mean shit when it comes to Internal Affairs." Cleary deliberately expressed a levity that seemed to relax his man. "But strictly off the record," he smiled a bit, "and this actually brings me to my point, I'd be surprised by anything harsher than a letter and a day off." Cruz depressurized. *Granddaddy always said to tell the truth.*

"But Monty," Cleary continued, leaning forward and magnetizing eye contact, "I don't give a rat's ass right now about that shit. I want to know about you, and your heart feelings about the ultimate decision you made to let that boy go. Everything else aside, is that going to keep you awake at night?" Cruz hadn't really thought that far. "'Cause you and me, we could sit here all morning and entertain 'what if' scenarios, like 'what if you'd let him drive and he pulled out right then in front of a family of four?'" Cleary glanced instinctively at the closest photo. "We'd be having an entirely different conversation, wouldn't you agree?"

"Yessir. Yes, I would."

"Yes, you would. But as that did not happen, 'what ifs' work pretty nicely for us. They provide, shall we say, a pleasant perspective."

"Yessir."

"However, given the unfortunate eventuality of your ultimate decision and hence our conversation this morning, your mind might start drifting off to 'if onlys.'" Cleary paused briefly in thought. "'If only I'd arrested, Brian,' I think you said his name was, 'a little girl would be alive today.'"

"She's actually in a coma, sir."

"You get the picture."

"Yessir. Sorry."

"And this is precisely the angle that fuckface at the Times is gonna focus on. Not that you let him drive home, not that he's underage; but, that a girl was hospitalized because he was driving drunk, and at some point earlier, you, an officer of the law, knew it."

"Doesn't matter that twelve hours had-"

"-no. Not at all. If anything, he'll focus on that as longer consumption time. No. Through his lifeless eyes and with his forked tongue, you'll be a fucking accessory by the time he's done."

William Cruz had nothing to say to all this. He generally tried not to fear what had not yet happened, and now was not the time to start. He still had his job, a position he enjoyed very much, with some of the finest people he'd ever known, present company included.

And from the tone of the meeting, it seemed he had not lost respect. That was enough for now.

"So, back to the original question. Do you harbor any gut reservations about your ultimate decision to release the young man?"

"No sir, I do not."

"Good. Preserve that, because once you begin questioning your first instincts, doubting yourself, you're through. Now, we can call it a mitigating factor for Internal when they review the case, whatever, but I am going to have you arrange a set schedule with Sheila for a time to make certain you are, and remain, fit for duty."

Sheila was the department psychologist whom Monty had complimented once on a new hairstyle. "You are so sweet. Wait'll my husband hears *someone* noticed." Monty since thought it best to lay off the attention to Sheila, though she'd never forgotten it.

"I think that's an excellent idea. I'll go see her now."

"Very good. Now, if there's nothing else, officer, I do have another appointment."

"Of course, of course sir," Cruz said, standing quickly, awkwardly, "and I do thank you for your time." Cleary stood too, and they shook hands over his desk.

"Stay strong, William. You'll be fine."

"Thank you, sir." Cruz went to the door, yet waited a moment before opening it. There was one more thing. "Sir?" And he continued when Cleary looked up. "When Macbeth was King of Scotland, it was said that 'those he commands move only in command, nothing in love.' My granddaddy taught me that quote. You, sir, are not Macbeth."

Cleary stared, dumbfounded, then smiled broadly and shook his head. "Officer Cruz, get the fuck outta here."

"Thank you, sir," and Cruz closed the door behind him.

Cleary was still smiling. *And above everything else, the brother quotes Shakespeare. A better man you will not find,* though a mental note was made to keep an eye on Lisa at the next party. After fifteen years of marriage, she'd claim to find that sorta crap sexy in a man.

14. Brian's Journal Entry 1

Saturday, early evening

Mom suggested I start journaling. She's always said, "Brian, you express yourself beautifully on paper," that I have a certain "penchant for the pen." I don't know. I've been talking to myself a lot today. I've been answering myself too, holding complete conversations. *Doing alright, Brian?* Nope. Still shitty. How's yourself? *Pretty shitty, man.* I think she's afraid I'm schizo.

If I could plead insanity you wouldn't be reading this. I'd be trying to stack unshelled peanuts or dancing topless to Jim Nabors and taking 8000 mg of Seroquel.

No. There's no plea for what I've done.

So, I will put my pen to paper, and write, for "journaling" is a made up word.

We are social creatures. We are not meant to be alone. I am alone. Dusk is falling and evening shadows are stealing across my empty bedroom: my single, frameless bed here in the corner, beside this schoolhouse desk over which I stoop; there, my dresser, with peeled paint and fading Bazooka Joe stickers with mismatched drawers and ancient cast-iron wheels. Here, timeless gouges in the dull wooden floor from Tonka trucks and the free weights bench; there, faintly sun-bleached geometric shapes and constellations of thumbtack holes on the walls of since-removed posters and pennants, a visual time line of boy to man.

Gleeful voices of children travel from several blocks away, like from a different time zone, jumping that last ramp, singing that last song before Mom has to call them one last time for dinner. The hoo-hooing of a mourning dove. How grossly symbolic.

I am alone. I am not away at summer sleep-over camp where I know no one. This is not the first day of kindergarten. I did not just drop that fly ball in left field. Those were probably lonely times in my life, and I probably felt an emptiness, a hurt, a longing for something, but I was not alone. Mommy was going to pick me up, the school bus was going to take me home, and it was Coach Dad who slapped my butt when we ran off the field at the long inning's end. Even when Gabrielle and I split I was not alone. I still had Jason, and there were plenty of other girls.

But now. This. Stan told me not to do anything crazy, like drive, or drink and drive, or drive and not return, because if Greta dies there'll be a warrant for my arrest and should I not be found I'll be declared a fugitive, plastered across *America's Most Wanted*.

Jason and I watched that program together just last Saturday, drinking a shot of bourbon every time John Walsh pointed at the camera.

There are no doctor's notes, no conferences to be scheduled. Jay can't act as an alibis; Stan can't sweet talk any DA. I am alone. If Greta dies, I go to prison. Prison, not jail, for an extended stay. A bit longer than summer camp. More like five summers, if the prosecution goes for voluntary manslaughter. If Greta dies. I never even knew this person, yet her death determines my life. I actually do have one thing, though, besides my health that is. At least I still have *if*. There's hope in *if*. Everything in my world now depends on *if*. On one fucking conjunction.

I was not of sound mind when I hospitalized Greta. I was very, very drunk. In fact, I was in a blackout. The last thing I can recall of the evening was meeting her, bringing her a drink. A vodka Red Bull. I know I made one for myself too because I was double fisting when I walked up to her. Then there were the lights, the cell phone in my hand. Apparently, I was the one who called 911, though I don't remember that either.

The boys, we always laughed about blackouts, recalling mid-afternoon of the next day or piecemeal throughout the next week the crazy things we did, and "if we didn't remember it, it didn't happen." That was our disclaimer.

I don't remember this, but it did happen. The blood tests taken this morning will verify my BAC, once they are returned from the SBI crime lab for my trial.

Blood tests, however, do not measure sanity, and renowned psychiatrists and certified medical examiners do not diagnose "very, very drunk" for the defense. Every bottle is stamped with its own little disclaimer that has roots dating back to when man first crushed grapes, a reminder as widely known as the caution that MacDonald's serves extremely hot coffee, so unless Stan the Man can prove that my ingestion of buckets-full of ethyl alcohol over a thirteen hour time period yesterday was unequivocally involuntary, I am a sane man in the eyes of the justice system.

But there is no sanity to be found in any of my recent actions. I drank and drove, then was given a gift. I returned that gift for door number three. It led to the cellar, where still I drink. I asked Jay to drink with me this afternoon at the river, and I asked Jay to stop by the liquor store so I could drink into this night.

I do not deserve Jason Braswell. He is one of the innocents dragged down those cellar stairs behind me.

It is now madness for me to crawl and scrape on all fours, ragged and torn, back through the lip of that fallen bottle that created the darkness, the living dead controlled by a thing external, but I need to find hope outside of *if*. Hope, other than the textbook standby of my "good health" which, ironically, is working against me. I have all my faculties while Greta Ann Mackenzie is traveling, visiting places external, alone.

That bottle will sap my health, will help me sort things out. There *must* be something.

Besides, mommy, I am scared. Dad? Help me. Won't you, please? I have a fear greater than I have ever, ever known, and I really want to wake up now.

In my junior year of high school I did a project on FDR and the Great Depression, and for it I read his First Inaugural Address in which is found the famous quote, "we have nothing to fear but fear itself," citing a "nameless, unreasoning, unjustified terror" in the hearts and minds of the American people. The speech was clearly motivating during that time of such futility, questioning the true essence of *why are we scared?*

He went on to say, a bit farther down, that "only a foolish optimist can deny the dark realities of the moment." That one was for Brian.

For there is so much hate towards me right now, wrath and ire from people I've never met. They curse my name. Or, maybe they're not there yet. Maybe they're still stupefied, dumb-stricken, erect life-images of Greta's prostration.

They are grieving. Grieving and praying.

Perhaps they have always been prayerful people, holily devout, bent on forgiveness of sins on earth, that all judgment will be rendered in the hereafter. Perhaps they are fire and brimstone snake handlers.

Or perhaps, now, they have lost their religion, are feeling forsaken and are screaming *why?* Or, perhaps they never had religion, and now never will.

The pertinent questions, though, are not ones of what, or if, they believe. None of that really matters now. In reality, it boils down to a question of justice versus vengeance. And here is where Jason will be tested.

I do not deserve Jason Braswell.

Tested. Shit.

These words are lovely, dark and deep, but I have promises to keep. And one is now to my best friend who for the past day has probably been caught between Scylla and Charibdes over the sociology test. So with this I conclude my "journaling" for the evening, to make a call to Jason and then to dead-man's float atop many a tumbler of Crown Royal, entertaining "perhaps maybes" and "ifs" until I exit this reverb, the starting gun of a long series of worst days of my life.

15. The Family Chat

Beth did have a way of being intrusive, abruptly in your face like the lonely housewife neighborhood gossip, which might have been attributed to her drinking except she always drank so I couldn't tell otherwise. Beth had a Type B personality and was extroverted to the extreme, and seldom did she adjust her bubbly charisma to fit the situation.

With Beth it was either all, or all. At least she was consistent.

I was able to handle Beth's zeal today. I was in fact ready for it. I needed to share, and this time it was Beth who met me when I returned from the river with Brian, glass still in hand though needing replenishing, scotch-flavored water on smaller rocks. She took my arrival as an occasion to do so, and I nodded when she casually asked, "You?" We took our drinks to the backyard, and she was skipping around like she had to pee. Beth loved news, in whatever form.

"So?" she asked as we sat at the picnic table.

"Where's Dad?" I began. "Car's still in the drive." I knew he was somewhere in the vicinity, walking the dog probably. Dad didn't have friends to pick him up.

"I don't know, Jason. Probably walking the dog. If he were in the house we'd know it by now, so hurry up and spill it while there's still time and the inquisition begins." Beth often slammed my father, but while it was uncomfortable I couldn't defend the man because she said what I felt.

Beth already knew the facts from the website video, and we'd watch the 6:00 that evening for any further developments. After that, and tomorrow's Morning Times edition, we both agreed the media play would relax as neither Brian nor Greta were celebs or held noteworthy positions, like school principal or youth minister. An assistant manager at Silver Bullet or a random junior at Brinkley were not news. They didn't sell papers. They didn't boost ratings.

I did tell Beth particulars, that Brian had blacked out and had been drinking an awfully long time and had drunk beer and liquor, and even liquor with an energy drink, he thought. No, he did not smoke pot, and yes I was very sure. Yes, he had lost his license, for thirty days at present. The trial would determine more. No, he had no plans to go back to his apartment. He needed his parents for rides. Yes, he was planning to keep working, depending upon if he still had a job. His mom thought that was best, to keep his mind from idling.

Beth agreed, though she asked if his mind were an engine.

The front screen door slammed and we heard Bill's holler, "Hello?" and Beth quickly took my hand. "Jason, whenever you need my car just let me know. Please, okay? I don't have pressing things to do this weekend and if something comes up I'll just call one of the girls."

"Thanks, Beth. Better finish this."

"Jay, re-laaax. Just stay put. He won't say anything." Beth said re-laaax to Dad an awful lot---*Bill, re-laaax, will ya?*---and her gentle admonishment to me was an instant pacifier, a reminder of the apple and the tree.

"Oh, huh. Here you are. I was just out walking the dog." Dad sat on my bench and smelled my glass and looked at his watch. "Beth gave me a little information on Bri-an, but I still have some questions." Dad said Brian's name slowly, deliberately, as if he'd been practicing it.

"The news video can probably sum it up for you better than I can, Dad, and it'll probably be on again in an hour and a half with the latest. Other'n that, can't really help you. I wasn't there."

"No, you weren't. Good thing I didn't eat a second bowl of ice cream, otherwise I wouldn't have heard the phone." Beth crunched hard on an ice cube. "But what the hell was the boy doing over on Safe Haven?"

"He'd just met Greta and was driving her back to school."

"To Brinkley? Christ. I'd think Maple would have been faster that time of night, from the Country Club. Don't you, Beth?"

"Well, Bill, I don't know what traffic situations hold at 2:30 in the morning."

"I dunno. Seems there'd have been a better route."

I closed my eyes and breathed deeply through my nostrils. The sun was still strong for that time of day. The birdies were still chirping, too. Pretty chirping, little birdies.

"Anyhow, I took some ribs out last night to thaw and I was thinking that, Beth, you could do your salad."

"Okee-dokee Smokey Joe." Beth had a lot to teach on patience and tolerance. She must have been listening to the birdies too.

"And Jason, if you'd shuck the corn we can look to eat about six." Again Dad smelled my glass. "You like that stuff?"

"Not really," I said, and drained what was left. "Too much ice."

"Heh, heh," Dad chuckled, clapping me on the back, then proceeded in some made up imitation, "So, dere, why-ya-drinkin'-it, dere, dere.." and trailed off in a grumble. "So, all set. I'll be in my study if you need me."

The dog was taking a monster shit on the lawn. So much for the walk.

"Oh, that's what I forgot," he said in an about face, snapping his fingers, purposefully striding back lest he forget again. Rarely did Dad leave just once. "Jason, remind me please to call Joe Markowski this evening?" First name basis, now. This was great. Maybe they'd become friends, go do guy stuff. "He called again today. Any thoughts?"

"Nope, nothing comes to mind. Maybe wants to congratulate you on a job well done with me." I didn't have the strength to get into it.

"You're kidding," he said with complete incredulity.

"Yes, dere, Bill, I'm kiddin', dere, dere...."

"Uh-huh, okay then, very well. I'll be in my study. I said that already."

"You said that already."

16. Jason's Take

I had a lot of time today for what my mother calls "reflection," a new-age term for deep thought, and having ample subject matter

I've come to terms with the fact that I am a lonely individual. Not necessarily today---as a bored kid wants a playmate, because Saturdays were usually either hit or miss with me and Brian, from his work schedule to our respective "chib calendars," mine usually being empty---but lonely, in general.

Chat and Jed were good for the party, the "go-to" guys, but neither could ever be taken seriously. At the age of eighteen they were slacker pothead telemarketer mall-rats with zero life ambition or intellectual curiosities outside their pathetic microcosm of Spencer Gifts and *Jay and Silent Bob*. I think Brian kept them on speed dial simply to complete a social picture.

Jed and Chat would revel in the limelight of Brian's new found notoriety, freely declaring in bad boy fashion how "they were with him that night" and spinning the yarn. The primary reason why they'd call Brian today would be for information.

So really, outside Brian, I walk alone. I have no other true friends. I return clothes to the mall by myself. Not that guys call each other to do such things, but that might be a quick stop to or from a guy thing, involving Budweiser tall boys and guns, like paint ball, or hunting deer.

A few years ago the church had a father/son softball game and cookout. On the few Sundays I went to church it was announced, in the bulletin and on fliers and by the priest at the conclusion of the services, well in advance of the event, and Dad and I never discussed it. It never appeared an option; though really, perhaps in justification, I would have wound up embarrassed anyhow.

So why bring it up, right?

A masking-taped strike zone on the garage taught me how to throw tennis balls with accuracy; the limitless sky strengthened my arm to snag my own thrown pop-fly baseballs. I caught sunfish in the university pond and garter snakes in our backyard fields while Dr. Braswell played professor.

Finally, after what seemed like hours of accumulated "in a minute"-s, we finally went places together; but never, it seemed, for a very long time.

I've always shied away from striking up conversation with him because I haven't known how to. A casual starter, like "What's up, dad?" could very well have him questioning, "Up? Up. Hmmm, let's see," giving him yet one more thing to think about.

Today, though, I really could have used my father. Today was his opportunity to be a dad instead of a guidance counselor or, better, a complete jerk, yet I was once again treated as though my situation and my friend were less-than and took secondary importance to a host of priorities, like shucked corn and ribs with Bill's Famous BBQ sauce.

I drank Dewar's White Label Scotch Whisky into the evening. I did relaaax, and Dad didn't comment. I overheard Beth pull some Jedi mind-trick on him, like "Bill, the boy's not drinking in excess," when he confronted her about it in the kitchen, and he seemed to interpret that as acceptable grounds for a seventeen year old son of an alcoholic to consume hard liquor, period.

Far easier it was just to fold, to choose inaction: the easier, softer way.

Dad did call Mr. Markowski and left a message, "Hi Joe, this is Bill Braswell returning your call...," and I smirked at the first-name basis; at my sudden thought of him continuing with, "tag, you're it"; and out of relief that I was afforded maybe one more night to muster up some sort of explanation for the egregious errors of my ways.

I was confident that had I the test in my possession I'd boldly go where no man had gone before. I had promised myself that, test in hand, I'd be up front with my father. I'd pull the telephone line and hide the clocks and lock the door to his study and send the dog to the pound and give Beth an outfit to return---completely free his mind of all distractions---and, dammit, I'd talk to the man. We'd sit down at the dining room table, in straight-backed chairs so as not to get too comfortable, and after introductions we'd dive immediately into the heart of the matter. For hours. We'd discuss everything. I might even learn where he was born.

I was reminded of Wimpy, who forever told Popeye, or Olive, or whomever, that he'd "gladly pay them Tuesday for a hamburger today." Hell yeah he would, and he meant it, too.

It always sounds so good when it is promised *today*.

The phone began ringing and, just knowing it was Markowski, I downed what was left of Beth's elixir and I skipped into the kitchen to do the dishes, a random act of kindness as a mitigating factor during this difficult time.

Damn, Brian, you fucking promised.

17. Saturday Night in 103

Marissa Alvarez called Tom and Emma Jean Stiltson when it wasn't too early to call, and, after an incredibly brief and digestible account of the tragedy, asked them to bring some of the Mackenzie's personals, including the little black phone and address book "which should still be on the coffee table."

Mister Tom and Miss Emma had been long time neighbors, were in fact recently-made- grandparents by their two daughters, Paige and Allison, who had both babysat Greta. The Stiltsons were already on the shady cul-de-sac in Braxton when Robert and Margaret moved in eighteen years ago, newlyweds, in their experienced eyes; newly parents; and newly homeowners. "It was all so exciting," Miss Emma was fond of recalling. "It tickles me to think how quickly we all hit it off."

The last time they were at Flint Regional, in fact, was the time they were looking after Greta Ann---they always used both names---for the day, and she fell from the tree Paige and Allison used to climb. "Broke her arm right in half, she did, and boo-hooed in my arms like I was her daddy," Tom tells at block parties.

"And you loved that little blossom right back like she was our third," Emma proudly chimes in. "Tom always leaves that part out."

Black book in hand, Marissa Alvarez then called the five family members Margaret Mackenzie had checked off: Grandma and Grandpa Pennyworth in Sacramento, Grandma Mackenzie in Toledo, and Auntie and Uncle Glover in the Hills, which was closer to the hospital than Braxton.

The three first-generationers all caught the next flights out, naturally at bereavement rates, trembling from palsy and nerves and repeating, both aloud and to themselves, *this is not the way it was supposed to be.*

ICU 103 had become a shrine. When all the relatives arrived, Margaret and her sister drove back to Braxton for Greta's room, her porcelain dolls and rag dolls and her gnarled one-eyed teddy; and framed bureau-top photos and framed wall-mounted collages and photo albums and school annuals; and posters of boys and posters of unicorns; and her music box with the spinning ballerina doing an arabesque, an heirloom from Grammie Pennyworth.

And finally, which they lay gingerly and with great precision over the sleeping child, the Laura Ashley comforter she'd bought with her very first paycheck.

And together, in ICU 103, they kept vigil, the Mackenzies and the Stiltsons and the Pennyworths and the Glovers.

They took turns reading *Make Way for Ducklings* and *Blueberries for Sal*; and Margaret hummed bedtime tunes, and smoothed her daughter's hair.

And the machine pumped 100% Grade-A oxygen.

And Robert paced to the machine, and wrung his hands and sat and paced to the sucking machine, and everyone had sudden flashes of recollection and realization, moments of fit and outrage and despair as they remembered the time when.

They cursed, loud and deep. They abhorred the machine, they loathed the drink. They condemned the boy. They damned God. They went to bed last night in thanksgiving and prayer, only to awake in an intestinal casing of offal and refuse. All that just yesterday held promise and fortune was now in the taloned grip of winged creatures soaring over steamy desolation.

The Mackenzies and the Stiltsons and the Pennyworths and the Glovers had been abandoned, and they cared nothing now for the time-trial of justice. Justice was not blind.

The boy named Brian Dildy, the demon responsible for this heinous crime, was still alive.

They had been wronged. They wanted revenge.

Bob lay his hand on the outline of his daughter's foot. Margaret had her face planted in her neck. Possibly asleep.

The others had slipped out. They felt they still had time, with the gentle guidance of Chaplain Honeycutt.

The staff for the most part was sympathetically gentle and respectful of space, though Bob could have done without that cold bitch Roxanne in Registration, who entered all the information on Greta's COBRA medical plan and said she'd contact Coastal Auto for them; but who also focused on and repeated three times the names of the responsible party, Robert and Margaret Mackenzie. *Correct?*

Bob cursed Roxanne for planting the seed that really did put a cap on the length of "Greta's stay," for she had truly become just a serial number on the side of some air pump. Every compression of that horrible instrument increased their out-of-pocket percentage, despite auto and medical and the paltry $15,000 life insurance policy, which had actually matured just this year through the Grow-up Plan.

Bob and Margaret had meant to up her policy, just like they'd been needing to update their will.

But, there had always been tomorrow.

Bob Mackenzie rubbed his daughter's foot. *We've got tonight. Who needs tomorrow.* That song line had always comforted him, Bob Seger he thought it was. It did little now, but it was something. He hummed the tune aloud in cracked fashion, singing it in his mind.

I know your plans don't include me.

Robert cried *Jesus* and fell at her feet.

Margaret moved her head, just a little.

The machine sucked.

CHAPTER THREE
SUNDAY

1. That's Jed Fishing

"Braz."

"Jed, whassup playa?"

"Ain't nothin' but the birds and the bees and the trees, my man. You?"

"Same, same. Just chillin', studyin' for soash and watchin', what am I watchin', I dunno, some shit on manatees on Animal Planet. Nothin' else on Sunday night. Did you know the early explorers thought they were mermaids? Mermaids. Fuckin' *Shrek* mermaids, you ask me." I was drunk from the day and nervously long winded because I knew Jed had called to fish. This is not to say he was heartless. He was just quite far from concerned. We'll just say he was interested. That's fair.

"Studyin' for soash my ass. Dildy finally gave up that test you guys bin yammerin' about?"

"Yep. Yep, that he did." The phone ringing last night was not Markowski, but Brian, offering the test and apologizing for its delay. The guy apologized, and my reaction was to lie, to tell him I hadn't thought about it. At all, in fact. I even acted surprised when he mentioned it. At least I might have acted contrite, might have said "dude, listen, I feel horrible telling you I *have* thought about it, and that's not right with everything you got against you." That would have been honest, perfectly called for and within the parameters of the understanding of our friendship. But no. I lied, when there was no reason to lie, and I built myself up to be something greater. Jason Braswell, you oughta be in sales.

"So anyhow, Jed, what became of Hillary? Gonna meet her parents?"

"Dude Jay, girl had a mouth for a 'Hillary'. Save that language for an Angel, or a Candi with an 'i.'"

"So, she's out then."

"Hells yea. And not a thin thing, either."

"Gogglin'."

"Big time beer goggles. So Jayman, listen, what's the skinny on Brian? I've heard all sorts of different shit, man, like he fled from the scene and was finally taken down at the Wal-Mart. Even heard the chick was decapitated."

"Jesus, Jed. Watch the news much?"

"Naw, man. Evening news is too fuckin' depressing."

"Jed, all's I know is what sells, man. Only new development is that she's been deemed comatose. Pick up a paper, man. It was in today's, front page." Indeed it was. The three pictures were of Brian's senior portrait, probably Greta's too, and of the crash scene, grainy but understood.

"Jason, I know all that, man. I was just hopin' you'd offer up an inside personal slant, is all. Worried 'bout the dude. Him and I go way back. Grew up together, even. D'jou know that?" Jed was using "together" very loosely. From six until they were too cool to go they saw each other maybe bi-annually, spring and fall, at their fathers' Kiwanis family fun days.

Brian said John Hedley senior was a stoner as well, and even today, at age 47, he still answers to his esoteric nickname, Jed Head.

"Yeah, Jed, you guys bin tight awhile."

"Yeah. See, think I oughta get my facts straight for my meeting tomorrow with the insurance people."

"Again?"

"Craziest shit, Jay. Din't I tell you? Meant to. Real reason for this call. Anyhoo, some bozo from Coastal called tonight to schedule a personal sit-down. Called tonight, Jay. Fuckin' Sunday. Can you believe the balls?"

"You're the telemarketer, there, Jed."

"Shit, even I rest on Sunday. At any rate, dude wants to talk about Greta, like I even know her."

"Talk about what?"

"He called it some 'final cursory information' so they can properly file her claim. Said it shouldn't take but twenty minutes, but it was important we meet immediately. You'll probably get a call too, Jay, either tonight or tomorrow."

A lightbulb went on. "Yeah, probably will."

"Yeah. So, Jay, I figgered at least you'd know if the girl's still got her melon so I didn't look like a total idiot in the interview."

2. Beer on Sunday

So it was beginning. The first shots had been fired. I *had* received a call from some insurance company that same evening, during the dinner hour, only a very disturbed Bill abruptly yet with terrific satisfaction hung up with a "sorry, he's not interested." Surely it was Coastal, and surely someone *else* would be calling back that evening, I informed my live-in secretary, so I'd be answering the phone if it rang again.

It was also a good little arrangement should Joltin' Joe try one last time, *Shucks, Mr. Markowski, he just stepped out*, another cowardly postponement of the inevitable. I had my test; it was time for that talk I promised myself. I wonder if Wimpy ever actually paid up.

Bill would find out, if not from a phone call then from the report card, the fact that I was habitually absent every Friday and most Thursdays, and that my best-scenario C would keep me from Dean's List.

This was my struggle, my daily torment, the monkey on my back.

This might be what kept me drinking, that Sunday.

The loads I carry.

I had picked Brian up today at twelve. He looked like he'd been lagooned, like he'd even already lost some weight. There's a sick idea for a diet plan. He still wore the air of Friday night. His charcoal mug said boxcar. His forehead was creased from play and rewind, folding and unfolding from torturous *if I'd only* scenarios. His unkempt hair was pompadourish. His lips looked kneaded and ruddy-sucked.

We bought beer. We bought beer and went to his apartment to once-over the joint; you know, to pick up a bit here and there and to open some windows, and we knew that it was gonna be hard so we just went on ahead and said, "Fuck it," and we bought beer.

Sometimes you just have to say fuck it and buy beer. At 12:00. On Sunday.

So we bought a twelve, because we knew it was gonna be hard, and went to Brian's apartment. I parked next to Roz. We each cracked a tall boy at 12:00 on Sunday, when there was no football to watch. 12:03, the digital read. After noon, now.

"'Least it's after noon," Brian justified. "Only alkys drink 'fore noon, ya know." He reached for a second.

"Sunday, Bri. Can't buy it 'fore noon."

Church-goers were returning. A few of them eyed suspiciously the two characters sitting outside 23-B.

The haggard one sarcastically raised his bottle, *salut!*

The neighbors purposefully made their way up the stairs, *don't look back, dear.*

"Can't buy it, no, but an alky'd find a way to get it. Sneak into the grocery store bathroom, quickly slam a few. Heard of a fellow who drank Listerine and fuckin' cookin' extracts 'cause he couldn't make his liquor last from Saturday night."

"Dude, that's just urban legend, like the dumb momma who named her twins 'or-ón-jello' and 'le-món-jello' because that's the first thing she was offered."

"Dunno, Jay. People do some fucked up shit."

"Like namin' your daughter Tequila, but spellin' it Te-key-la, like that's supposed to make it okay."

"Teller at the bank's named Chablis. Think I met a Chianti once, too."

"It's the black folks that do it. Wonder what that's about."

"Braz, Whitey's just as guilty, dude, namin' their kids after cities in Texas and last names as firsts, like Taylor and Tyler, and Mackenzie." Brian shook his head as he mentioned Mackenzie. "And inventin' new spellings for all of them because everybody's gotta be a fuckin' individual."

"Not if you're I-talian, namin' all your boys Petey and Paulie and all the girls Marie."

"Danger there, though. Fuckin' wind up whackin' the wrong dude. 'Looka wutchoo dun, you fuckin' goombah. You whacked the wrong Paulie. I tole' you to do Paulie. Paul-IE, da one wit da fuckin' -IE, not da one wit da -EY.' Bada-bing, bada-boom. Pow."

Brian smiled a little. Not much, but I did catch a trace of a smirk. I rubbed his shoulder and shook it a bit. "Let's get into character," I said, and opened my door, worried about a call the nosey neighbors might have made.

"That's 'Jules' from *Pulp Fiction*, and we ain't about to get into character, we're gettin' out of it. Shit, Jay. What the fuck you gonna do without me when I'm gone?"

I felt like I'd just been slapped very, very hard.

3. Cleaning the Apartment

The apartment looked as though its occupants were instructed to vacate the premises immediately. Dinner dishes still lay sink-side, forks and chop sticks stuck to plates in congealed hoisin and Sambal and misfit bamboo; baby corn and pea pods abandoned in filmy brown wok-smear. Beer bottles of different ranks, Bud to Sam Adams to Amstel, were strewn about like Easter eggs, labels mindlessly peeled off and tightly twisted into toothpicks or ripped apart and balled into BB's. Maybe a third of the bottles were empty.

Shameful waste. We shook our heads.

CD cases were used as coasters, which really pissed Brian off, and the remote control was in the potted begonia. Evidence of my consumption had dried in abrasive patterns in remote areas of the bathroom as projectile-splash from the bowl. The football helmet was in the dishwasher. The After the Fire disc was snapped in half, from Brian's exasperation at my wanting to hear *Der Kommissar* a third time, it dawned on me.

The simple fact that Brian Dildy---whose toilet water was blue, who regularly dusted the top of his refrigerator, who actually parented a potted begonia---had allowed his apartment to reach this stage was evidence alone that he was not of sound mind when he left that evening.

Just last weekend, this procedure was a time of fond reflections, of laughter at our folly and cringing at our near misses, which was always what they were and what they always would be.

We were invincible.

We were indefatigable.

We were insatiable, with miles to go before we slept, and our compulsion never stumbled over checkerboard memories, vomit, or hangovers. If anything, they added flavor to the story.

But this afternoon I felt dejected, humbled, silently cleaning out our dressing room like the second place band in a reality television series.

Gosh. And we had come so far.

This wasn't hard. This was excruciating.

"Brian, this sucks."

"Gotta git er done, Jay." Brian's ass was sticking out of the refrigerator, rocking a bit as he sponged up beer spilled from a tipped bottle that someone had saved for later. "Not like me to let it go this long."

"Understood, and normally I'd be Molly Maidin' right alongside you. But in light of recent circumstances, we need to be tossin' a ball, maybe sparrin' a few rounds. This shit can wait, Bri. Our minds need to be elsewhere."

"Hence, the beer, and I need another," Brian was reminded, slapping down the sponge and wiping his brow. "And Jay, you need to know," he continued, tossing the twist-off cap into the garbage, "that from now until the gavel strikes there'll be no more 'laters' for this guy. See, fact is, when she goes, I go, Jay. Tomorrow's no longer a fuckin' guarantee."

"Alright, given, but you yourself said that if, *IF* she dies---and it still is 'if,' by the way--- and you're arrested, you'll be out the same day on bond. Your word, dude, straight from Stan." I drank from my beer. "And then, no! Listen, man, dammit!" Brian had tried to interrupt. I had the conch. "Then, you got, what, three, maybe six months until the shit goes to trial? Way it looks, now, from what you told me, you've still got plenty of tomorrows, Brian."

"Jason, you've missed the point completely. Zoom." Brian's spread hand waved over his head. "Don'cha see, dude? Tomorrow, or Thursday, or six months from now, my goose is cooked, 'cause she's done, dude. She's comatose. She's holdin' that fuckin' ticket, just a-waiting at the station." He brought it down a notch. "And I carry my phone on vibrate *and* ring, right by my side, not for that call from some blonde fox in a thong but from lawyer Stan, tellin' me a warrant's been issued, to pack it up."

Brian closed the refrigerator door and began, perfunctorily, wiping down its dustless top. "It's like the man who's got twenty-four hours to live decidin' to take a nap. I got things to do, man, and no offense, but playin' catch ain't one of them."

"So what are you gonna do?"

"Like I said. I'm gonna clean my apartment, and I'm gonna send your ass to my bathroom with some Ajax and a scrubbie to do your part. And I'm gonna drink a lot of beer, and you're gonna drink a lot less 'cause you're drivin'. And together, my friend, we're gonna ruminate over heavy matters until I can't see, and then you're gonna drive my drunk ass home, at which time I will, finally, allow myself a nap." Brian finished a tall boy in three swallows. "So? How's about them apples?" His eyes were carbonated-red and bleary, and he released a fantastic belch.

"Gonna hafta make a run now, then. Beer's almost gone already."

"Well, then, Hopalong, we'd better get ridin'."

4. Brian's Journal Entry 2

Sunday, dusk

The journaling this evening may be a bit illegibible. I am a drunk man. The room is actually spinning a bit. Been a long time since that's happened. Thought I'd moved past that stage.

After we finished cleaning my apartment---what the whole point was in that I have no idea---and as I settled comfortably into involuntary bottle-to-mouth automation, Jay less so because he was driving, the conversation launched straight into other people's reality.

I wasn't about to confront my own. Jason can claim it, via his father. But hell if I do.

Hell no, certainly not now, if ever. Why? Why even delve into the notion that I am an alcoholic, and therefore quit drinking, when there is a very good chance I will soon be segregated from everything societal and introduced to a subculture where well over half the population were under the influence when they committed their crime. Why go sober? I'll already be enough of a minority as it stands.

Quitting drinking now would be like that man taking a nap. I gotta get it in. If Greta dies, I'll have plenty of time to confront an addiction.

Shit. Please don't die, Greta. Please. I want to call you "sweetie" and I want to hold you, cry over you, breathe life into you or at least be able to visualize all this but you remain human clay, an unprepped department store mannequin. Featureless.

We had no connections. You were nothing to me.

A random passerby on an inner-city street.

The object of a serial killer.

It's starting to sink in and I'm losing my cool. I'm flaking off inside, like mica. I want Dad to put me to bed, to tousle my hair and say "buddy, it's gonna be okay" like he used to do whenever things got bad. He was always right. I want Mommy to wake me up with song, *Good morning, good mor-ning, you, slept the whole night through*. I want to love this person who drank vodka Red Bull. I want our parents to go to operas together. I want us to wear matching sweaters.

Please. Blink the sleep from your eyes, lick the crust from your lips, wiggle the scratch from between your toes. Twitch from a dream. Smile from a memory. Be.

Greta, I don't want to go to prison. I don't belong there. Since high school my two worst fears have been sharks and prison, and from the comfort of any room with a view I have watched *Predators of the Deep* and *Lockdown* with morbid curiosity, confronting my nightmares then switching the station with relief.

Phew. Hate it for them.

Wanna avoid getting bitten by a shark? Simple. Stay out of the water. Any dummy can tell you that. Surfers know the gamble, that one day their board might be the silhouette the great white mistakes for a seal.

I knew the gamble too, Greta, and I gambled often. Every time I drank, it seems, I surfed with sharks, because drinking and driving was an art and I had it down. Just look at me today. Living proof, with barely a scratch.

I am so sorry.

Officer Cruz, I do believe you are a piece of shit. No, now, hear me out, because I know at first I was grieving over your Mexican ass but now things are piecing themselves together.

I should have been breath tested. I should have been arrested. It should have been a long afternoon, for both of us.

I should have been arrested and gotten out on unsecured bond, and I should have gone to drunk classes, and I should have paid a shit load of money for limited driving privileges for a year.

But you needed to play good cop, didn't you, to win me over. Or maybe the procedure was too much for you on that beautiful Friday. Had other plans, maybe, that involved fried and glazed dough rings and coffee with the boys. You sorry son of a bitch. You're the reason crime's so high in this country. You get paid to enforce the law, not suggest it. Pig.

And while I'm at it, fuck you too, Stan. Stan. What the fuck kind of name is that? You were probably born a "Joe" but felt you needed to pick up a geek name with the geek, pound me in the ass profession you chose. Stan. What have you done for me, anyhow? What in the hell are we paying you for? So you say you've been schmoozin' with the bondsman, getting the paperwork in order for my quick release and talking him down to 10%. And you've arranged with the po-po and the magistrate that you'll pick me up when the warrant's issued, to cut down on shock value.

And let's see, what else. What else is there, Stan? I've done everything for you already, haven't I. You just need to collect.

You haven't been a lawyer. You've been a travel agent, making sure it all goes smoothly for my extended vacation.

I'm done for today. No word yet, on anything. I'd like to think she's one day stronger. Maybe tomorrow after school Jason would be willing to go by the hospital, do a little Perry Mason for me.

Jason. He really is a great friend.

5. Brian's Dad

"Brian, are you awake? Hey, Bri?"

Bri. My only son. My sweet, sweet boy. How much I wish to say it's been good to have you home, to ask if you want to do stuff for old times sake. Wanna go on the trail? Maybe bring our knives along too, do some carving in some trees? Don't tell Mom, though. You know how she worries.

I did the best I could, son. We both did, your mother and I. The talks began when you were young, six you were, when I went away for the first time. You and Mommy visited me, and you said the place was "paradise" because of the stray cats and the unlimited soda and the volleyball court sand in which you played, a litter box for the stray cats. My job sent me to the place to get well when I crashed my car between the two great trees at the beginning of our trail. Your car seat flew through the front window, but you were not in the car. Mommy ended that only a week before.

My job sent me to the place to get well, but I did not get well, and six weeks later I was arrested again and I lost my job and I lost my driver's license and I went away again, this time to live in a Home with other men like me. They call it a halfway house. You visited me there, too, but it was a scary place. No place at all for children.

All this you remember, I know, because I've kept it alive inside you. I haven't allowed you to forget the months I spent away from home to get well, and the many nights I'd suddenly leave to resume. The questions you were asked by your elementary schoolmates when their parents read it in the papers, several different articles, you in turn asked me, unabashedly, because you knew you could.

Daddy, were you in jail? Katherine in my class said you killed someone. Why did you do it if you knew it was bad? Can you still drink root beer? Can I drink root beer?

"Brian? Buddy?"

When you were seven you created a Top 10 list on How to Make you a Better Person. You just did this, on your own. I still have this list.

1. Never drink beer or anything with alcohol in it again.
2. Think twice before drinking and driving.
3. Do not ever do drugs.

I like number six: never drink sea water or you will see stuff that is not really real. You have always been such a neat kid.

Damn I love you. There hasn't been a day gone by that I haven't told you, or thought about it. When I first started in the Program, had about three months' serious clean time, a fellow told me he and his boy still said they loved each other, still gave hugs. You were seven then, around the time I guess that you made the list. I was thirty-five. Randy was about forty-eight, I think, and his boy was maybe nineteen, a bit younger than you are now. I felt so relieved to hear it doesn't have to go away.

Bri, honey, I never entertained the notion that my talks and candor would make you immune. There's too much out there that Dad and Mom can't compete against. It was my everyday hope, though, that I'd allow you to see that the thing that very nearly destroyed everything that is me was quite possible in you too.

And I'm not even saying now that you've got it, but you sure as hell are lying in a place where I should have been many, many nights.

"Brian. Wake up, Brian."

It is my place to say that if I could take this from you I would. I would. Sitting here today, fourteen years sober, I would take it if I knew it would save you. If the Good Lord appeared and said, "Take this from thy son, for he has reached his bottom," I would do just that, for I know about bottoms.

Because Brian, love, I too have been through hell. I have seen the monsters.

I have seen the twisted faces and have heard the cackles and screams that would have any man institutionalized, confined.

And I have been institutionalized, but the monsters have the keys to those doors, too.

Yes, Brian, I have been through hell. Did I ever tell you how it got so bad for me that I drank mouthwash and vanilla when my supply ran out? I can't remember. You've heard so many scary stories. But we never think it's going to happen to us, do we? We never stop to think that one day, in one split second, the "other guy" might just be me.

Brian, I have indeed been through hell, but I kept going. I know about bottoms, and unfortunately I too know how necessary they are for the alcoholic to quit. For good.

I know about bottoms, but I also know about salvation afterwards.

If it was guaranteed that the shit would stop now, with the last drink you took that has distilled the air in this room, then I would let you sleep. I would go downstairs, and I would tell Stan that permission has been granted to take me instead.

"Brian, son, wake up. Now. It's time to go."

CHAPTER FOUR
MONDAY

1. Braxton Girl Dies

A nineteen year old Braxton girl died last evening after a single car accident on Safe Haven Road early Saturday morning. Passenger Greta Ann Mackenzie, a rising junior at Brinkley University, suffered severe head trauma when her vehicle collided head on with a tree. Ms. Mackenzie was not wearing her seatbelt.

The driver, Brian Christopher Dildy, 20, of Meadowmont, was released this morning from County Jail on $100,000 secured bond. Mr. Dildy has been charged with involuntary manslaughter, in addition to the preliminary charges of DUI, reckless driving, and driving while having consumed alcohol under the age of twenty-one.

If convicted of the Class F felony, Mr. Dildy would face up to sixteen months in prison.

Prosecution is allegedly seeking a stiffer penalty.

State legislation has recently been passed for stricter DWI/DUI penalties, including heightened fees, increased license revocation periods, and longer prison terms for repeat offenders.

Grassroots organizations like MADD and SADD have been instrumental in championing the bill.

"Innocent people, from infants to elderly, are dying, and countless lives are shattered," shouted Glenyce Wright at last month's demonstration at Town Hall. "This runs far deeper than mere carelessness and irresponsibility. It is the 8th Deadly Sin!"

Ms. Mackenzie was placed on life support Saturday as the result of brainstem herniation as family and friends paid their last respects.

Services will be held at Dodd Funeral Home in Braxton on Thursday at 2:00.

2. The Markowski Talk

I could have gone straight home after the sociology test, but I had made up my mind that enough was enough. No more games. Brian had his closure for the day. I needed mine, too.

Joe Markowski was packing his briefcase with the last of the exams, of the stragglers who used the entire three hours. These were the ones who attended the SAT prep class for personal enrichment, the ones who actually studied their notes for sociology. Having finished thirty minutes ago---I had actually finished in half the time, but wanted it to appear like it meant something to me---I milled about the halls until time was up.

"Mr. Markowski?"

"Yes, Jason."

"Think I could talk to you about a few things?"

Mr. Markowski smiled. *This oughta be good.* "Calls worked, huh?"

"Yes. Yes, I guess they did, Mr. Markowski," I said, clearing my throat, studying him. I pulled up a desk. He sat behind his.

"I guess I've got some explaining to do, here, and I'm not quite sure where to begin." I looked at my teacher for a prompt, a head nod or something. Nothing. He just reclined in his swivel, hands clasped around his neck, and stared at me with a smile. The man appeared to be enjoying this already. "So I guess I'll just, uh, begin, then." I wanted to make like Benny Hill and slap him a few times on his bald head. *Say something, dammit.*

So I drove right into my confession, surface-detailing half-truths for my end-of-week truancies that sparked no reaction from my audience, and the more he stared the more I gabbed, exposing now the fact that it was Brian Dildy I kept company with, as if he didn't already know, and that we occasionally drank alcohol, as if he hadn't already guessed that.

Either I had all the makings of a star witness, or Joe Markowski a chief investigator, because the man got it all without ever saying a word.

Had he allowed me to continue, he might have heard about the first time I got laid, a dull, very brief event, more occurrence than experience but a confession nonetheless. Mr. Markowski showed mercy.

"Done now?" he interrupted between breaths, still smiling. The man, he sure could smile. Guy Smiley.

"Yes sir." I was wiped out. "Guess I've about said it all."

"Feel any better?" This was not going at all the way I had thought.

"Well, now, Mr. Markowski, that really depends. Should I feel better?"

"Shoot, I would, at least hoping the conversation would keep my teacher from calling my dad again. At least you tried, right? There is some solace in that."

I lowered my head. "Yea, a bit."

Mr. Markowski went to open a window, and stood with both hands resting on the sill, facing the ball fields. Another gorgeous day. "Okay, dumb question time now. How's Brian?"

"No such thing as dumb questions, sir." Markowski was not smiling, now. "Sorry. I, um, I don't know, truthfully. They took him last night, and again I'm not sure where I fit in, with pre-trial hearings and stuff. I just, really, I just don't know. Ya know?"

"Your question may have been rhetorical, but yea, man, I do know." My teacher said *man*. "I do. I might wear plaid and sensible shoes, and I might call my pants 'slacks' and I might, no, I *do* have male-pattern baldness," he scratched his crown, "but I too was twenty-one, and I too did some things that were, well, let's just say 'questionable' and leave it at that."

"Left."

"Yea," and once again he was lost in this day, and in yesteryear, and in condolence. "And buddy, how're you doing?" My teacher said *buddy*. "You've been through a lot, too, I imagine."

"I'm okay. I'm alright, but it's really not about me, you know-"

"-Bri-, I mean Jason, it is. It is about you. It's about you, and the Dildys, and the Mackenzies, and it's about the officer who pulled you two earlier that day" ---spooky, spooky man, to know anything about that last part--- "and it's about this community, and parents everywhere. It's about their own children, and possibly, like me, about the way *they* were." Mr. Markowski shook his head sadly. "We're all affected, Jason."

"Yessir."

"So, how are you doing, really?"

"No disrespect, Mr. Markowski, but again, I really don't know."

"You're a good kid, Jason. No disrespect taken." He clapped me on the shoulder and shut his briefcase, body language hinting that the discussion was ending. Hold on a minute, there, *buddy*.

"So, how'd you do on the test?"

"I think I did okay. Sure studied hard for it. Had a lot of ground to cover, you know."

Mr. Markowski was smiling again. "I'm sure you did fine, Jason. Most of my students seem to do very well on the final." He gave me a quick wink, still smiling. "Suspiciously well." He moved his brow like Groucho Marx.

"Oh, and Jason. You can go ahead and tell your dad that you and I got everything straightened out, okay?"

"Absolutely okay. Thank you, sir."

"Yea, yea. Didn't really want to talk to the man anyhow," he mumbled to the door. "You know, I came to Premier as an English teacher, but six years ago the Powers gave me sociology, *gave* it to me, because they knew 'if anyone could do the job, I could.'" He laughed. "I've learned a lot, though, like, statistically proven, the best times to call people when you *don't* want to get them are, believe it or not, at mealtimes. Someone did a study. They just know it's someone trying to sell something, and they don't want to be bothered."

"You've got my dad down, though I think he was looking forward to your chat. He doesn't have a lot of people to talk to."

Joe Markowski turned off the light in the room and guided me out as he shut the door. "I might be a stodgy old bird, Jason, but there's a reason I'm in high school." He winked again, and playfully punched me on the shoulder. "Use me, okay? I'm here."

"I will, Mr. Markowski. Thank you."

3. Anecdotal Evidence

"Jason Braswell, was that you?" the voice called from the front office as I passed, and the sound of the secretary's purposeful stride click-clacked quickly across the checkered linoleum. "Jason, hon?"

"Yes, ma'am?"

"Jason, good. There's a gentleman here to see you." She looked around, then whispered as if in gossip, "A detective." I figured Ms. May was a tad confused as I was still expecting to hear from the insurance guy, and surely the police were not that quick off the mark.

But sure enough, unless Coastal believed their agents needed holstered weapons, the brass had arrived.

"Mr. Braswell, hello," the very tall man said, turning from feigned interest in the school's fire evacuation plan, and I was immediately reminded of Special Agent Crawford from *Silence of the Lambs*.

"Hello."

"The two of you can sit right…in…here. There we go." Ms. May one-arm guided us into the conference room, expeditiously and without commotion so as to preserve the idyllic little haven that was Premier High. The detective's presumption led him to have his tape recorder with microphones already planted in the center of the table, alongside a pitcher of iced water with two cups.

Accommodating, to make for a better witness.

"Mr. Braswell, I am detective Glenn Scott of the MCPD." He held out his hand, and I shook it firmly. "And let me first begin by saying that you are not in one ounce of trouble." He waited for me to exhale. "Because, most kids, once they see the gun, get a bit nervous, begin thinking they'd done something wrong." The guy didn't even need Celebrity Look-a-Like. He was a dead ringer. "So, then, why don't we have a seat, and I'll tell you a little bit about why I'm here."

I was certain from my silence I'd already been pegged as a little shit, but I had entered some sort of foreign survival mode that was going to make it difficult for Crawford here. *I know my rights, you bastard.*

"Sir, I am familiar with why you're here."

"Good. That's great. Then I'm going to-"

"-however, for my own protection and because I am new at this, *I'm going to* need to consult my attorney." Of course, I had no attorney. If I had one, I probably wouldn't have been "new at this." Surely I had just become a little shit wise-ass.

The detective smirked. *I'll play.* "Mr. Braswell, you understand you are not on trial here."

"Understood, Detective, but my best friend is, and I will not incriminate him further, especially not on tape, until I speak with legal counsel." I took a sip of water. "With all due respect, sir."

"No offense taken, Mr. Braswell. I in fact appreciate your candor, and your very limited knowledge of the way things work." No, he was younger than Crawford. Maybe Alan Shepard in *The Right Stuff.* Definitely same actor, though. "So here's my card," he continued, sliding one out of a pocket fold designed for very important people to preserve their cards. "Be sure either you or your 'legal counsel'---what's his name, out of curiosity?"

"Javier Rubenstein." No clue where that came from.

"Unh-huh. Right." The detective began collecting his equipment. "Well, be sure to contact me in the next couple of days, Mr. Braswell. I'd hate to see this unnecessarily develop into something scary, like obstruction."

"It is my right to remain silent, Mr. Scott, unless-"

"-then Mr. Braswell, until you are willing to cooperate I'd strongly recommend you do just that." He gave me a don't-fuck-with-me glare that made me just about shit my survival mode.

4. Gotta Have a Reason

"Wyoming. Here's a new one. Never met anyone from Wyoming," he said, comparing picture to face. Up, down, up, down, hands it back. "What's Wyoming known for?"

"Cheese." Shit, that's Wisconsin. The guy looked at me funny, but left it alone, figured *dude's from there, he oughta know.* I slapped down the $7.40 exact change I had nickled-and-dimed from Bill's armrest depository and I brown bagged it to the store to pick up the Monday edition.

The meeting with Detective Scott had given me a fourth reason to drink that mid-Monday morning, my plan since dawn: to take the test, to speak to Markowski, to buy a paper then begin a pint. My intentions were to watch the morning news; however, I awoke a bit ragged from yesterday's beer with Brian and last night's generous Dewar's nightcap, without Beth, reasoning that what she didn't know couldn't hurt her [support of my drinking.]

I needed to keep my allies intact, after all, during this difficult time.

I checked my phone. One message, from Dad reminding me he needed the car by 1:00 and to buy gas, that he usually went to the BP on Sunset, near the cleaners.

I uncapped the bourbon and took a deep deep swallow.

I felt the warmth go all the way down.

That was very, very nice.

The car behind me honked. Green light.

I drove on.

5. Carl San

Carl Davis was an angry young man. Skinny, pock-marked, with thinning, gel-spiked hair and a pronounced Adam's apple his friends called his "goonie," Carl looked like a barnyard rooster. He knew this, and it pissed him off.

Carl was a high school dropout from a broken home. His step mother was a crack whore, his father an abusive alcoholic. Three children, none of them kin, crawled and tottered around on the thin brown trailer flooring in day-old diapers. His real mother died giving birth to his brother, a drooling wheelchair cripple in the special class. Fetal alcohol syndrome.

Carl hated alcohol. It pissed him off.

Carl Davis had heard about the job at Silver Bullet through his mall buddy, Jed Hedley, who told Carl that he was friends with the assistant manager, and would put in word because he knew they really needed somebody. (Jed included the fact that, of course, he'd apply for it himself---and would get it, because he was "in" with the assistant manager---but that he detested physical labor. Thus, he sniffed out the telemarketing lead fellow mall buddy Charles "Chat" Parker had provided, and he'd never looked back.)

Carl knew he could clean cars, could even impress some people if they'd just leave him the hell alone.

See, Carl Davis also had a bit of a problem with authority. He hated taking orders, and the people who gave them really pissed him off; especially on this day, when one person in particular wasn't on the clock, and when he'd been drinking alcohol.

A few empties were under the seats of assistant manager Dildo's seats, and that wasn't ginger ale in those sippees. No one drank soda so ambitiously, even on a hot Friday afternoon.

Don't like the way I'm polishing your shit mobile, Brian San? Let me just put this vacuum head through your taillight to give you something else to think about.

Dear Editor:

You should be interested to learn that I am first hand witness to the fact that Brian Dildy was drinking early Friday afternoon, and that everyone now knows that he was stopped by police for a broken taillight. Why would the officer let him go when he openly told the cop he had been drinking? Brian himself told this to a good friend of mine. He seemed proud of it. Something should be done to protect our world of these criminals.

From,

Concerned Citizen of Meadowmont

Jeremy Stevens

"And, so, Blake, that's what I have. This is the second time I've heard about this---the first was by email on Saturday afternoon---so there's got to be something to it."

PD Spokesman Blake Sharpe was ready for this call, had prepared his talking notes from a very detailed conversation with Monty Cruz. *A good man*, Sharpe thought, *to come clean with this early*. Saved him a lot of headaches. Saved the department some embarrassment as well.

"Now, are you gonna toss me a bone, here, Blake, or make me dig?"

Sharpe refused to dignify this recorded telephone conference with any first-name-basis crap. He and the editor would never have that kind of relationship. He summoned the closest officer to be witness to the call, and he proceeded to give the bare facts in laundry list fashion and as they were relevant solely to the public domain. Anything speculative was simply "under review," and there it would remain indefinitely.

And when he was through, he answered the editor's questions, though if it wasn't already provided there was absolutely no expanding.

"So the driver was impaired at the time of the pull."

"That is under review."

"But surely he acted impaired, Blake."

"Negative."

"Okay. And you said Officer Cruz allowed the man to drive home after it was obvious the man had been drinking."

"Officer Cruz followed the man home after he detected an odor of alcohol on the driver's breath. Affirmative."

"And is this MPD procedure, to allow a person to drive a motorized vehicle after the 'odor of alcohol,' as you put it, had been detected?"

"Negative." Sharpe did not need to go into detail with this as he included it in his verbal public record. The editor was just being a prick.

"Has Officer Cruz made it practice to allow individuals to drive who had been drinking?"

"That is under review."

"Blake, come on now. You're not giving me much to go on."

"I'm giving you the facts as you need them." Blake Sharpe had dealt with this creep so many times and knew of his affection for playing with words, so often dancing around libelous extremes with the most minute, albeit tape-recorded detail, eagerly putting into print exactly what one said and not what one obviously meant to say.

Case in point: last year a rookie was cornered by the Rag editor following a shootout on the lower east side, and he made the statement that "every officer doesn't know Spanish" when asked about the communication barrier. The confusion with the semantic paradox of *all do not* and *not all do* was blatant, so incredibly obvious because the rookie himself often acted as an interpreter; but they were, nonetheless, words spoken by a credible source and were therefore anonymously quoted as "one police officer attested to the fact that–."

Needless to say, that single falsity created a ripple that resulted in humiliating backtracking and diminished faith from the ever-increasing Hispanic population.

Sharpe knew the editor already had his story and had already formulated an opinion that would soon become gospel. This call was about adjectives and adverbs---show don't tell, living color---and correspondent Blake Sharpe wanted no involvement in the Monty Cruz case becoming dirty laundry.

6. Cut to the Chase

"So what happens now?"

The two sat in Stan's car outside the courthouse, having just completed the pretrial hearing. "Now it's time for you to begin demonstrating how truly penitent you are."

"Like, what. Apologizing? Sending flowers?"

"No, Brian. You know that's not 'like what.' Look, I know you're a mess right now and I'm not going to fart around with sunny side-up pep talks. This is bad. The grim facts are, you're guilty, and you will be going to jail. Right?" Stan leaned over for an acknowledgment. Brian met his eyes. Good enough.

"Right. And to further complicate things, the prosecution wants voluntary, and PD will more than likely hop-to with a very, very thorough investigation to get attention off the Cruz bungle.

"Dickhead."

"Fine. And finally, unless, oh, I don't know, the nineteen members of the grand jury spontaneously combust, they will return a true bill, and you will be indicted, and arrested again."

"Just like that."

"Just like that. We've been through all this, Brian."

Yes, we had, but when it was all only an "if."

"This is a very high profile case, and there are a lot of angry eyes staring at it." Stan paused to watch a tight-skirted businesswoman high-heel it across the street. "And besides, it's a popular saying in the legal circle that the grand jury would indict a ham sandwich."

Oh, you lawyers. Real gassers, you are. Brian rolled down the window to spit, but some deputies were buying hotdogs from the cart-man. Fearful of being seen soiling a city sidewalk, he decided to swallow. Brian didn't need to give the people any more leverage.

"And what about bond? Should I begin saving now for another ten grand?"

Stan sighed. "Truly, Brian, I do not know. I've already begun talks with the DA and the magistrate's office about 'if' scenarios, hoping to convince them early that you aren't a flight risk." He rolled his window down too, creating a cross breeze of wieners and kraut. "But, while everybody's hustling and bustling, getting paid to do their jobs, there are a few things you could be doing on your own behalf; again, to demonstrate to the court how truly penitent you are." Brian remembered these as mitigating factors from a previous talk.

"Like AA"

"Yes, for starters. Alcoholics Anonymous recommends ninety in ninety. I urge at least one meeting a day until your case is heard, and that you get signatures for verification. You and I can devise a form.

"Additionally, you'll need to have an alcohol assessment performed. This is a procedure required by the State, and I'll help you get started on that. And then, finally, a good amount of psychological counseling, to help you with your current difficulties in addition to culling out any, um, underlying themes."

Immediately Brian again thought of the insanity plea, but after playing the whole tape through he dismissed it as insane.

He was screwed. Jail time, or more jail time. Like leading the lamb to the slaughter.

"Let's just say, Stan, purely hypothetical of course, that I don't do these meetings or this counseling. Where'll that put things?"

"Of course, and inaction on your part is definitely an option. First, you'd make me look like an idiot in the courtroom, but I'd soon get over that after a hot shower and dinner in bed in front of Dancing with the Stars, with my wife rubbing my tummy to help digestion.

"You, on the other hand," and he tapped Brian firmly on the shoulder to bring it home, "would be viewed as cold-hearted and callous, and without a modicum of regret all twelve angry jurors would unequivocally sentence your ass to the full sixty-four months of the Class D felony, DWI, and reckless driving charges."

Judging from his reaction, Stan didn't much appreciate the hypothetical.

7. Chat

The front door was open when I pulled into the driveway, I'd have thought for ventilation on this day designed for spring cleaning except the storms were still up. Knowing his M.O., Dad was getting anxious, quick-checking the road with every irregular sound as if that would hasten my arrival, once again certain I'd been born without short term memory.

And that was almost confirmed, for remembering I'd forgotten the damn gas I pulled right back out, nearly sideswiping the very fine real estate agent stepping out of her Le Baron, obviously there to show the house next door.

116   *Jeremy Stevens*

Might have to stop by when I got home, be neighborly. Perhaps bring a plate of Entenmann's.

And how old are you? she'd whisper as she finalized the sale.

However old you want me to be darlin'. I woo-hooed out loud, took the pint to half-way, cranked the Nickelback and sped off to the Shell station right down the road.

It was a b-e-a-utiful day.

"Professor."

"Lady Chatterley, what's the word?" Chat was leaving the Shell with three gas station hot dogs, the kind that rolled on aluminum tubing beneath a sneeze guard. His were already shriveling.

"Bird's the word. Where ya bin hidin'?"

"S'only Monday, Charles." He gave me his *you-know-better-than-to-call-me-Charles* look.

"Dig, dig, but a lot's happened, man. Figured we'd've heard from you."

The gas nozzle clicked off and I hung it up. 12:50. Had to move.

"Talked to Jed just last night and he told me about the insurance people. You get a call?"

"Professor, the only thing I was witness to Friday night was Saturday morning. Fuckin' woke up with about fifty swizzle sticks stickin' outta my nose, man. Felt violated. What the fuck game was they playin'?"

"No idea. Listen, I gotta make waves. Lemme call you tonight. Cool?"

"Cool, do that. An' here," he said, putting his food on the pump to better reach into his deep pocket. "Altoids. They're 'curiously strong.' Take the tin, in fact."

"Damn, bloodhound. That bad?"

"Detectable. These'll at least add a minty freshness to the sour mash."

Good for Chat. I jumped in the car, tucked the pint in my waist, tightened my belt, and popped five mints as I knew when I got home it would be touch and go.

I felt like I'd just had a Vick's Vapo Rub throat culture.

Dad was out the door as I pulled into the driveway and the woman was again getting out of her car. I felt part of some conspiracy. "Hey, where'd you go?" he asked, putting a box of papers in the backseat.

"Exam, dad? Remember?"

"No. Ten minutes ago you pulled in, then left again. You almost hit the car insurance woman," he said, nodding in her direction.

"Huh. Hitting a car insurance woman. How's that for ironic."

So that's who she was. Not real estate at all. Okay, then.

"Are you with us for supper?"

"Let's not plan on it, alright? Mom said something about-"

"-did you remember gas?" He turned on the car and stared at the panel.

"Excuse me. Jason Braswell?" she asked hesitantly, like a woman who'd been hung up upon and almost run over by the same party. Yes, she was beautiful, definitely not a mom with those features, and we were about to be alone in my house.

The sun, it sure shone brightly on this day.

"Filled her up, even. Good for you. Oh, Jason, this is---" Dad snapped his fingers, trying to recall.

"Jennifer Dwyer from Coastal Auto Insurance, Mr. Braswell," she said to me, reaching out her hand.

"Jennifer. Right. Okay, Jason, I'll see you for dinner. Beth's doing her chicken." Dad shut the door and pulled out.

"Rightee-O," I responded to Jennifer, whose hand I might have held a bit too long.

8. Coastal Auto Insurance

I felt the veranda a better location for our little rendezvous as there was a slight breeze that would help the Altoids mask my odor.

Drinking sure was taking a lot of effort, planning and all.

After one more hard pull I hid the bottle and put in some Miles Davis and got two Cokes, one with lime as that's how Jennifer wanted hers, and I met her on the porch with the tray of drinks and some Pepperidge Farm Mint Milanos I knew Beth wouldn't mind if I borrowed.

I coolly asked Jennifer, whose silky Pantene hair was now pulled back save a few incredibly sexy strands I just knew she'd left dangling for the lust factor, how long she'd lived in Meadowmont.

She coolly replied, "I don't. Now, is that 'Braswell' with a 'z' or an 's'?"

Given, that was an important question.

Truth be told, I had no idea where we were to go with this, what it was this liability adjuster was out to find. I figured it was all just red tape formality, the "i's" that needed to be dotted before any legal settlement could be made. And my assumption was 100% correct, only through some fancy guesswork a mere five minutes later it dawned on me: *These people ain't payin'.*

"Did you witness Greta Mackenzie giving Brian Dildy the keys to her vehicle?"

"No, I wasn't around for the actual transaction-"

"-but you did say that she appeared cognizant of the fact that he had them."

"Sure. He was holding them in plain view."

"Okay. And again, for clarification, Greta Mackenzie was cognizant of the fact that Brian Dildy had been drinking that evening."

"Cognizant is really the wrong adjective to describe any of us that evening, Ms. Dwyer-"

"-did she know?"

"Yes."

"How did she know?"

"They drank vodka Red Bulls together."

"Then she was cognizant."

Suddenly this woman wasn't so beautiful anymore. *Gimme my cookies back.*

"Okay, Mr. Braswell, just one more question, for clarification purposes." She sipped from her Coke with lime. "Did Greta Mackenzie appear under duress, coercion, or threat when she left with Brian Dildy that evening?"

And it dawned on me. Jason Braswell, you are a rat. Your testimony is going to be key in the ultimate complete denial of the Mackenzie claim, and here you are, singing like a bird.

A drunk rat-bird. A buzzard, you are.

"Mr. Braswell?"

"Huh? Yes. I mean, no. I mean, she went willingly. She even offered me a ride."

Jennifer Dwyer jotted a few more final notes in her pad, crossed a few more t's, closed her case and got up to leave. "Mr. Braswell," she concluded with outstretched hand, "on behalf of Coastal Insurance I would like to thank you very much for your cooperation this afternoon."

And for helping us save hundreds of thousands of dollars in car insurance.

I took her hand. "Ms. Dwyer, do you enjoy your job?"

"Very much I do, Mr. Braswell. It's a great stepping stone to the next big thing."

"Which is?"

"Litigation."

9. Moment of Clarity

I allowed Jennifer Dwyer to see herself out, and having poured what remained of the pint into a water bottle with very little Coke, and with a back-issue of Rolling Stone headlining the original Pink Floyd my plan was to nap in the backyard hammock. The stresses of this day were far too great for mere mortals, and it wasn't quite 2:00.

My entire body also felt as though I'd been shackled to kryptonite for the past hour.

Beth had bought this ridiculous collapsible foam-rubber hammock mat from Brookstone, the nirvana of over-priced non-essentials, which added a zero-gravity feel to my already insensate mass. There was the requisite, distant sound of lawnmower, a trace of Miles bellowing out the last of the cool. The afternoon felt climate-controlled. The fresh air blowing, as if from a fan atop sauna hot-rocks, tired the bugs. I felt like I could be poured.

Brian and Greta were on hold. I was powerless over the situation. They had each determined their own fates that evening, had each stood at a turning point as Brian had described it. Brian didn't have to get laid. Greta's arm wasn't twisted to do anything. She nodded. He drove. She died. I hate it for him, but the ice-cold base truth was that he fucked up.

And she did too, though who'd dare even think that now.

There wasn't a single thing further I could do for either of them, so I sucked again from the water bottle and read the first paragraph from Rolling Stone for the fifth time.

What is it now? Man, just let it go. Everything is relative. You've just taken an exam, made a difficult confession, narrowly averted a legal testimony and were seduced into a second. You've already worried about where to hide it and how to disguise it, and you'll be alone now for a good two hours to ride out the finished pint.

So at least enjoy that ride, man. Set sail.

Then somehow it was inserted, somewhere between moderate coherence and the pre-sleep jerk, the one thought that caused me to bold upright in an *oh shit* panic, that sudden weakness like blue lights in the rearview or the teacher catching you cheating. In one fluid motion my torso raised and my legs threw themselves over the side of the hammock before my somnolent mind was ready. I began to snake to the house with no formulated purpose other than to do something, because I knew it had been done and that it could not, right now, be reversed.

Maybe in a good two hours, but not right now.

How in the hell could I have been so careless? I began pacing and tapping things, pulling at my hair and repeating "no, no, no," hoping for that a-ha moment, *remember, dude, you threw it out at the Shell station.*

No such luck, because I didn't.

I needed something to go on. I called Dad's office under the pretense of something I'd make up if he answered, just to hear his voice and gauge if there was need to panic. Of course, he did not answer. He was in class. *Oh man, what did I do?* I called Chat on his cell to ask him if he'd seen me throw anything away, but it went right to mail. I was desperate for something.

Think. Backtrack. I'd grabbed the pint from beneath the seat and so cautiously tucked it beneath my belt. I grabbed that liquor bottle, pulled it right out from that brown paper bag, possibly sliding out with it the receipt of purchase.

Yup, that's what I did alright. Yes indeedy.

An open brown bag, creased only at the folds, deliberately placed beneath a seat for covert access. Crumpled into a ball, well, I could defend that as most anything. That might even have rolled beneath the seat. But the open bag told a whole lot more.

This was hard evidence. And the receipt sent it home.

10. The Family Afterwards

Christopher and Catherine Dildy were doing yard work when Stan returned from the courthouse with Brian. They'd both taken off from work, for the week in fact, and wanted to go with Brian to the hearing but he wouldn't have it.

And they didn't contest much. They knew Stan would take care of their boy.

Catherine was in the flower bed and Chris was spreading mulch around their newly planted dogwood when they pulled up, and Stan didn't stay to chat though they'd all gone back a ways. Stan tooted as he pulled off, and the Dildys waved, and clapped the earth from their hands, and through his mirror Stan felt their grief and a pain from his own helpless inability to do anything more consequential for the family whom he'd known for so long.

"Darling, I've some lunch prepared. Your father and I would love it if you ate with us, but of course-"

"-no, Mom. No. I really need to be with you guys now."

And Catherine dropped her gloves---*sweet, sweet baby, come here*---and she hugged her boy, and she cried into his chest, though not like she used to be able to do he had gotten so big; and he cried into the top of her graying head, and he held her tightly, though not like he used to do she had gotten so frail.

And Christopher rubbed his boy's shoulder, a muscular shoulder he felt, and stared down at his five year old hand print in the cement and the childish spelling of d-r-i-a-n with a stick, and teared at the way things now had to be.

Lunch was special, Mom's fettuccine alfredo with sauteed shrimp, homemade focaccia and salad, not standard noontime fare but Catherine had had the time, and hoping Brian would join she wanted their time to last.

Christopher led the family in prayer, again not typical lunch procedure but they certainly had the time, and now a new inclination. "Heavenly Father, we give our thanks this afternoon for this food we are about to receive, together still as a united family. We pray for those who are suffering, particularly the Mackenzie family, and we pray for Greta's safe passage to Your House. We pray for forgiveness of our sins and transgressions. And finally, dear Lord, we pray this day for the desire to please You, for the desire to do Your Will. It is in Your Name we pray, Amen."

They began in silence, and Brian knew it *was* his place to break it because Christopher and Catherine, his parents, deserved the consideration.

He knew they were not waiting for an explanation, and he knew what he said would not be countered with rebuke or inquisition.

This was the suffering time. The penance had since begun.

"Pops, I'm gonna need to start going to AA."

"I'll bet."

"Yeah. Stan advised I go every day, maybe even sometimes twice a day until I go to trial."

"AA can be a powerful mitigating factor."

"You know, don't you, Dad."

"Yes, I know, son." Christopher stabbed a shrimp, wound up some noodles and slathered it with mopped-up sauce. "Really sorry these are the footsteps you're following in." He followed the enormous forkful with a gnawed off slab of bread so he couldn't say anything else.

"Chris," Catherine warned with raised eyebrows. *We agreed.* Christopher nodded, figuring out a way to chew.

"Guys, I love you so much. There's absolutely nothing you could have done differently. Okay?"

Chris nodded again, and from half the bite said, "Okay, Bri. I love you too." He swallowed and drank of his iced tea. "There are plenty of meetings around. In fact, there's an open meeting right over at First Methodist every weeknight at eight. I haven't been to that one in a while."

"What's an open meeting?"

"It's just as the name suggests. It's open to alcoholics, their kin and concerned friends, or anyone who thinks that they might have a problem. It's particularly attractive to those who aren't ready to say, 'My name's so-and-so, and I'm an alcoholic.'"

"You just answered one of my questions."

"Yea, Bri. That's a really tough admission for some people."

"Like comin' out of the closet."

"Yes, very much so."

Catherine Dildy had since excused herself to begin clean up, and used this pause to holler from the kitchen if anyone wanted coffee. They both declined. Too warm for afternoon coffee.

"So do you think I am, Dad? An alcoholic, that is?"

"Buddy," he said, cupping Brian's hand in both of his, "that is truly something you need to decide for yourself. A car wreck and manslaughter doesn't make it necessarily so." He felt his son stiffen. He caressed his hand with his thumb. "The fact is, it doesn't matter at all what I think. I can only suggest, and you're already committed to going to AA so I haven't got much else. Did Stan say anything about counseling?"

"He did, to see if there are any 'underlying themes.' His cute little way of tellin' me I need to find out if I'm mental."

"Cute or not, alcoholism *is* insanity, Brian, with roots that extend deep into some chasms that need exploration. Counseling helped me. A lot. Of course, I admitted I was alcoholic three years before I decided to do anything about it."

"You went to meetings, though, you said. That was something."

"At first, sure, it was something, but its luster wore off quickly once everyone saw that my true motive was to shut them up so I could keep drinking." Catherine came back in with a dish towel over her shoulder and sat down, one leg folded beneath her. "She'll tell you."

"I plead the fifth."

"Nope, not allowed. Weren't the meetings just a ruse for me, at first?"

"Honey, your father thought he had the world fooled. He was, for all intents and purposes, a self-centered, pompous ass. He wore his suit to those meetings after work, even though he had plenty of time to change beforehand; deliberately, I knew, because he felt he was better than all of them."

"She's right."

"I am right. And he'd lie. He lied all the time, even when he didn't need to lie. And he smelled-"

"-alright, alright-"

"-well, you did, and so did the whole house. There. I'll shut up now."

"And you stayed with Dad, throughout it all."

"Yes, Brian. Yes, I did." She got up and went to sit on her husband's lap. "I did. Because I knew, I just knew, that somewhere, buried beneath all that filth and muck, was the man I first fell in love with, and I wasn't willing to lose that good man without a fight." Catherine's eyes were red and watery now. She kissed Chris on the cheek and got up for a tissue. "And though perhaps you were too young to remember some of the crap, you stayed with him, too."

Brian leaned back heavily in his chair. "Well, I guess it's payback time, huh, Dad?"

"NO! No, dammit. We are not doing that," Catherine hastily interjected, as if she knew it was coming. "I will not have it, from either of you. I've seen your father through it, and I'll be DAMMED" ---she palmed the wall and a picture fell--- "if it gets you too."

She burst out in tears. "At least I know that in a couple of months you'll be in a place where the monster can't get you."

Brian stared at his empty placemat. Chris glided his finger around the rim of his glass. Catherine sniffled.

"Okay, I'm sorry for that. But Brian Dildy, please. You go to those meetings, and you hang on to every word those wise people have to say. Do you understand me? Because they all might smoke and look a little worn, but those who have been there a while have found a life that few of us know."

"Yes ma'am, I understand. I'm sorry I've-"

"-Brian, listen, got an idea. What say we make tonight your first meeting?" Chris suggested hopefully. "We'll grab a bite, a small one after *this* lunch, and go together."

"Now there's an idea, honey-"

"-actually, guys, I was kinda thinkin' about askin' Jay if he'd wanna go with me. I mean, I've never considered AA a father-son thing, you know?"

"Jay could come with us-"

"-Dad? Please, okay?"

Chris Dildy looked genuinely crestfallen for a second, but quickly brushed it off with a nod and a smile. Brian saw all this, and he hurt. "Let me just get my feet wet a bit first." He took his Dad's hand this time. "Deal?"

"Of course, deal. It is what it is. Just know I'm here, alright?" Chris patted Brian's hand and went to finish up with the dogwood.

It is what it is. This fact was very unsettling for the recovering alcoholic, who had recently lost all serenity, and the ability to accept some things that he could not change.

11. A Friend in Need

What reason would he have to look under the seat? Maybe to grope about for an umbrella, but the drought was forecasted to continue all week. The problem was, not only did he keep his car clutter-free, but Bill always noticed the things that didn't belong. He was great at finding misplaced items, like the ring of car keys you had just a second ago.

So, if the coins happened to fall out of his pocket onto the floor beneath his seat, not only would he need to collect them, for there was a place in the armrest for loose change; but, he would immediately see, and he would know---receipt or no receipt---what was wrong with that picture.

I knew where Beth kept her scotch and this would have been the time for it except I also knew I had to play sober responsible boy if I even toyed with the slightest notion of exoneration.

I had my story. If confronted, I'd confess with shame-faced regret that yes, indeed, I did buy a bottle of something brown today---I think it was whisky, but they looked alike to me I was so inexperienced with it all---but, good heavens *NO!* not for me, but for Brian, who was having a really difficult time.

I'd head-nod solemnly at the mild admonishments and reminders of the Brian-types, and innocently agree that while I was obviously trying to be a good friend, in the long run I was doing a lot more harm than good.

I predicted the conversation to then slide into how great the house looked, how very thoughtful it was of me to mow and vacuum and wash and dust, to even find time to take the dog for a walk, all quite naturally "random acts of kindness."

Of course, Beth wouldn't buy one bit of this charade, which was why it needed to be a father/son, closed-door session, for confidence, bonding, and sound advice from a recovering alcoholic.

This case could be won. I just needed to play, and not smell, the part.

But as I was unloading the dishwasher the phone began to ring and I was thrown right back into panic mode because I'd prepared my defense for a sit down tête-à-tête. Dad did not have caller id---in fact, he even still had a rotary-dial phone in his study---but he did have voice mail, so while the call went there I scampered to Beth's cabinet for just one more quick-nip of courage.

There.

It was Brian saying he'd try me on my cell.

My cell began to vibrate and I answered excitedly like his call was overdue. "Hey man," I said.

"Hey buddy, how'd the test go?"

"Funny, the answers just came to me. Musta bin all that studyin'."

"Musta bin." We laughed together. I was glad it was Brian. "Got back from court not too long ago. That was fun."

"Musta bin," I said. Space-filler titter now.

"Yeah. So listen, Jay, I was just callin' to see what you were doin' tonight."

"As of yet, Bri, book's open. Mom had said somethin' 'bout havin' supper, but she'll retire early. And I'm exempt from American History tomorrow mornin'. So really, it's free and clear. Whatchoo lookin' at?"

"Lookin' at askin' a favor, Jay."

"Shoot."

"Well, I need to start goin' to AA meetings, every day in fact, to have somethin' to present in court when I go, and-"

"-man, I'll be happy to drive you. What time we thinkin'?"

"Well actually, Jayman, there's one at First Meth, right on the corner over here."

"Oh?" The house phone began ringing again. *Sunnuvabitch.*

"I was hopin' maybe you'd go with me, you know-"

"-to AA? Brian, dude-"

"-just hear me out here for a sec, alright?" I did. "See, it's what's called an open meeting so you won't have to say shit. Just say, 'My name's Jason, a friend of Brian.' Or make up a name, or say 'no a-speaka Inglais.' I don't fuckin' care." I kept listening. The phone stopped ringing and had gone to mail. "It would really mean a lot to me, though, dude, if you came along."

"Brian, I don't know, man. It's AA. I have no place there. It has to do with that 'anonymous' part-"

"-dude, you gonna make me beg? Christ, Jay, it's one fuckin' hour and a dollar. And they'll have coffee, and Krispy Kremes even-"

"-Brian-"

"-actually, Jason, you know what? Forget it. Just fuckin' forget it, dude."

And with that, my best friend hung up on me.

He just, hung up. I couldn't believe it, but there it was flashing in front of me.

Call ended. Call ended. Call ended.

12. Bossman

"So that's your decision, then."

"I'm afraid so."

"And there's no other way."

"None. It is what it is, and corporate won't have it. I'd just assume git 'er done locally, nip it now, before they even need to ask. 'Sides, Nick, you oughta be excited, man. Assistant manager's a nice little pay raise for you, and no one's more deserving."

"Well, thank you, and I am excited. I am. But I hate it has to be at Brian's expense."

"Nick, don't get me wrong here, okay? I like the man. I do. But however you wanna slice it, the guy's a felon, a murderer. And my suspicions are he's a drunk as well. Arby's next door got a tip that he and a buddy were tossing empties into their dumpster Friday, the very same Friday he killed that girl about ten hours later. A drunk, I say, and I can't have a man like that representing The Silver Bullet, Nick. You understand."

Nick was disconcerted by two things, one, that the restaurant "got a tip" about someone putting trash where it belonged; and the second being that he was privy to so much speculation from the boss regarding one man. It made Nick wonder what was said about *him* behind closed doors.

But the fact did remain that he was about to become a salaried employee, still and forever at-will but salaried nonetheless. At whoever's expense, that was huge, and Nick certainly did deserve it.

The rap at the door was the end of the good news report, and Nick stood to shake Bossman's hand. "Congratulations, Nick. I've given you his schedule for the week. Just look on the board. And I'll have your new name plate for you first thing in the morning."

"Alright, sounds good, thanks so much," he responded smilingly, and he opened the door to stand face to face with their topic of conversation.

"Brian."

"Well hello there, Nicholas."

Nick couldn't tell what Brian knew, so he just outstretched his palms and shook his head and said, "I'm sorry, man. I truly am." That covered all bases.

Brian said, "No sweat, kid," even though Nick Staples was a good ten years his senior, and he slapped both of his hands in a low-five though that's not what they were there for. "Glad I could help."

Okay, he knew.

"Sure didn't waste any time, did you," Brian said over the new assistant manager's shoulder. "'Guilty until innocent,' is what you always say."

"Nick, please shut the door behind you-"

"-no need, Nick. I won't make a scene-"

"-you already have. Door, Nick."

"I came in to get my check, and I see a single straight line through my hours on the schedule. Straight line, deliberate like. Used a ruler and everything."

"Brian, does this all really surprise you? I mean, think about it. Part of your responsibilities here requires you to drive the customers' vehicles. I assume they took your license-"

"-who's the snitch?"

"Excuse me?"

"Buzz is, someone's bin havin' a little fun with me."

"Brian, you're newsworthy. People talk. It's what happens."

"You're a dick."

"And you're fired."

"No shit. Hence, you're a dick."

"Have you been drinking? Get out. Now."

The question pricked like full body acupuncture. His heat index felt a ten degree surge. He was heavy, dense like a beaten biscuit. His head blipped meltdown.

"Now, Dildy."

"I need my check." He swallowed the lump.

"You'll get your check once we get your shirt and name plate, or the $25 recovery fee, whichever comes first."

Although he never would admit it, not even to his best friend whom he didn't feel he had anymore, Brian left quickly before the bossman could see the tears.

13. Brian's Catharsis

This wasn't a cry Chris had heard before.

This wasn't a broken-finger cry, or a go-to-your-room-you're grounded cry. No.

This was a cry from a great intangible, blindly pulled from the magician's closet, the figurative void deep down there.

The hurting place, where middle schoolers play pranks on the new kid. Where first loves are lost.

Where twenty year old boys cry for their daddies.

Christopher Dildy drove without destination, deliberately, at or below the speed limit and coming to complete stops, through city streets and over highways to rural service roads with green sea pastures and red barns.

And Brian spoke faster, coasting through periods, quantum leaping between now and then, from admitting and apologizing and accusing to zigging and zipping and zagging. He freely used his favorite curse, the granddaddy of them all, as five of the eight parts of speech---*He fucking fucked me, the fucking fuck. Fuck!*---and he angrily tested the seatbelt, and he calmly smoothed back his hair.

And when he had worked himself to a panting fatigue, and his eyes felt pruned and his teeth sore from clenching and gritting, his father asked, ever so calmly, almost invitingly, "Feel like getting drunk?"

And Brian, thrown aback, came this close to lying, condition-response. *Not a "Dad" question here, folks.*

But he did not lie. It was all out there.

"Yes, I do. In the worst way." He looked at his father.

"Yes, you do," his father repeated softly, nodding. "Then Brian, I say we get ourselves to an AA meeting."

14. Jason's Telephone Chat

"Chatman Caruthers."

"Professor, what's happenin'?"

"Ain't nothin' but a thang like a chicken wang."

"On a string, havin' it yo' way at Burger Kang."

"Ice cold. So, Cap'n, I called to see wass on the itinerary for this eve."

"Jed n' I'r headin' to Slang's for a little fireside in his basement, pass around summa da good stuff. You game? Or di'jo breath give you away?"

"My breath din't, but my foolishness about did. Good thing Bill din't happen to check under the seat."

"Whatchoo leave, the bottle?"

"The bag. Still can't find the damn receipt."

"Never take the receipt, professor. Sign on the door says 'all sales final.' Receipt's just a paper trail, will find you sittin' in one a them twelve-step meetin's."

"Yeah. Hey, funny thing you should mention that. Brian needs to go, you know."

"I bet he does. A whole shitload of 'em, prob'ly."

"Yeah. He asked me to go with him tonight. For support, you know?"

"Yeah, I know. So you goin'?"

"Hell no I ain't goin', man. I'm not an alcoholic. Hello?"

"Yeah, I'm here."

"Yeah. So, okay then, 'bout tonight-"

"-it's pretty fucked up you ain't goin' with Brian, man. Cat's obviously scared."

"Okay, then, Charles-"

"-name ain't-"

"-Chat, Chat, Chat. Okay, then, Chat, you go. Listen, the entire fuckin' city knows the name 'Brian Dildy,' and everybody and everything associated with what happened Friday night. I go to that meeting, and pretty soon I'm an alcoholic too, an' I don't need that shit. You there?"

"Yeah, I'm here."

"They say it's anonymous, but Brian's newsworthy. And people talk, Chat. People fuckin'....chat, Chat."

"I don't know, man. Brutha asked a favor, an'-"

"-I've been favored outta my ass with questions and interrogations 'bout shit I've got no involvement in. This AA thing, though, is where I draw the line. 'Sides, dude, I got exams to worry about. It's fuckin' finals week, 'member?"

"Alright, Jason." He called me *Jason*. "'Syour decision, man. So long as I don' hafta live with it, my name's Paul, and it's between ya'll."

"*Pulp Fiction*, right?"

"Exactamundo."

"Bang, nailed it. So listen, about tonight."

15. Brian's Thoughts about Journal Entry 3

I don't know what I was expecting.

No. That's wrong. I know exactly what I was expecting. I was expecting yellowed shades rolled down over filmy fenced-in basement windows; rustlines streaked down cracked dusty brick from flaky leaky pipes in low ceilings with missing tiles; the static bzzzzz of single track lighting covered by cylindrical grating, flicking shocks like a backyard mosquito zapper.

I was expecting the smell of morning-after tavern radiating carbon monoxide, tar and sworn-off booze from weathered, beady-eyed and nerve wracked exoskeletons tossed randomly in corners or in clustered support groups.

I was expecting penetrating stares and murmurs, tisk-tisks and head shakes, finger pointing. *See? That's him, over there.* I was expecting commandments and "thou shalts," genuflecting at feet, subservience.

The only thing accurate in my visual was the basement, the outside stairwell of which reminded me of those leading to a fallout shelter. Figuratively enough, there appeared to be a light at the end of the dark angled tunnel. I was so glad I had my dad with me to guide me towards it.

Outside the door, leaning back against the wall in a collapsible chair holding a bottle of Dasani was a short, muscular, bald headed man with a sleeveless lumberjack, jean shorts and work boots. Both ears were pierced with hoop rings. He wore sunglasses. He had a gruff voice.

He looked like a bouncer, checking id's.

"Hello, there, stranger!" he exclaimed, rocking forward to greet my dad with a clapped hand and a hug. "Chris. You look great man. Absolutely fantastic. How's your pretty wife. Catherine, right?" I'd never pictured my old man holding a conversation with, much less hugging, a man who obviously rode a Harley.

"Catherine it is, Greg, and she's still just as radiant, thanks for asking."

"Cool, cool. That's cool, man. Name's Greg, man," he said to me, and he pulled me to him in like clapped-hand fashion. I wondered if he was about to bounce me off some ropes.

"Name's Brian-"

"-Greg, this is my son, Brian."

"Brian, great to meet you. Your dad here's a great man. First face I saw when I entered, eight years ago next Friday, Chris. Eighth blue chip. You gonna be able to make it?"

"Wouldn't miss it, Greg. Listen, we're gonna go get settled-"

"-go, go, please. Brian, pleasure brother." We hugged again.

"Pleasure's mine."

Greg must not have heard about me.

Here was a clean, well-lighted place. Here there was laughter around the coffee pot, a mingling of societies, a billboard for prosperous diversity: a Pierre, a Lamont, a Rosalba, a Logan; a lawyer, a doctor, a bum; a butcher, a baker, a candlestick maker. Most knew my dad by name, and my dad knew most. Ironically, it reminded me of the *Cheers-*bar theme song.

But when the gavel struck and the voice rung out, "All right, people, let's have an AA meeting," the talking ceased, the seats were taken, and with bowed heads we said the serenity prayer in unison.

"Dad?" I whispered.

"Yes, son."

"Should I say I'm an alcoholic?"

"What does your heart say?"

"I haven't heard it yet."

"Then wait. It's not time yet."

So I waited, and listened. There were a few preliminary readings that allowed me to grasp the simple idea of what this was all about, and a few words popped out at me---powerless, unmanageable, sanity, God---that made me think very, very hard about why I was in that chair.

There was one line in particular, one which made me shiver. *Half measures availed us nothing. We stood at the turning point. We asked His protection and care with complete abandon.*

I looked around. There were still a few smiles, but more now a concentration, an absorption, a serious stillness and a telepathy of which all seemed to be a part.

There was healing to be had here, that much was obvious.

And there were many, many stories to be told.

"Dad?"

"Yes, son."

"I have my answer."

"That's good, son." The group began introductions. It was coming around to us.

"Oh, and Dad? Sorry. One more thing."

Dad looked at me, put his hand on my knee, smiled, and winked. "I love you too, son."

The guy, he sometimes beat me to that one.

CHAPTER FIVE
THURSDAY

1. The Opinion Column

A teenager is dead, and a pall looms over the Meadowmont Community. It is an air of sadness, that one of our own is suddenly gone and that none of us had the opportunity to say goodbye. It is one of agony, thinking about the last words we had spoken, and wondering if they were kind. It is of fear, that the thing is possible, on any random day, at any given time, to any one of us. And it is anger, that alcohol is once again ultimately responsible for another premature death, at the hands of yet another premature drinker.

Yet, alcohol is not on trial here. Freewill has determined that. Brian Christopher Dildy made a choice. In fact, as we have come to learn, he had two to make that Friday: one, whether to drive *again* after approximately twelve hours of potation; and the second, whether to obey the Law, an option he had apparently been afforded approximately twelve hours before the fatal tragedy.

One does not need statistical evidence to comprehend the dangers of drinking and driving. One does not need to know, say,

that 41% of all fatalities last year were caused by drunk drivers; that 258,000 people were injured, or that the median BAC (blood alcohol content) for all these incidences was .16, twice the legal limit. One does not need to know that over their lifetime, one in four families will be affected by a drunk driver.

These facts are not necessary to logically conclude that drinking alcohol considerably increases the likelihood of the two-ton vehicle becoming a deadly weapon.

It is unsettling to hear that when Brian Christopher Dildy was pulled over for a routine traffic violation mid-Friday afternoon, and it was determined he had been drinking, he was given a warning and released. What exacerbates this legal gaffe, however, is that William Cruz III has since been described by his superiors in the department as "exemplary," "just," and "loyal." One even described the officer as "flawlessly thorough." While such adjectival felicitations would rule out one officer's pardon in the desperate hope of boosting ratings, they also hint at accepted practice. And this concept is, indeed, unsettling.

It is fact that, in 1980, thirteen year old Cari Lightner was killed by a drunk driver who, two days previously, had been released from jail for another drunk hit and run charge. As a result, her mother founded MADD. It is fact that the twenty-seven Kentuckians killed in a church bus in 1988 died at the hands of a repeat drunk driving offender. It is fact that in 2003, writer, cyclist, and webmaster Ken Kifer was killed by a drunk driver who had been released from jail only four hours earlier for a separate drunk driving incident.

And, these are facts: that, at 6:35 on Sunday evening, 18-year old Greta Ann Mackenzie was pronounced dead from a drunk driving accident in Meadowmont; and, that the driver, Brian Christopher Dildy, had been drinking earlier that day, as confirmed by a police officer who, according to his fellow lawmen, is "faultlessly thorough."

2. The Dodd Funeral Home

It was for their own selfish reasons that Robert and Margaret Mackenzie were angry with God, but they knew they could not renounce Him completely because their baby was now resting peacefully in His hands. If a Holy Parent Conference could have been held, perhaps some questions would have been answered and some tempers allayed which would have permitted Greta's final sending-off to have occurred in His house.

As that was not possible, however, they compromised, having their reverend deliver the service on neutral ground. Most assuredly, God would get the message, and He would understand.

The cars lined the streets of surrounding city blocks and parked illegally in the neighboring drug store and antique dealer's parking lots an hour before the 2:00 service in Braxton was to begin, and lunch-goers and quick-trippers were late getting back to work but they did not honk in annoyance or flip gestures, did not curse the congestion, but instead used the standstill for personal meditation and prayer.

Displayed on a sturdy easel outside the front door, on the green synthetic stoop mat and flanked by lilacs, was the ornately-framed portrait of Greta, cum laude, that the Mackenzies had removed from above their fireplace, a $850 expense that fully captured every nuance of her lust-for-life radiance. Inside the narthex were Kodak spreads of Greta, and flora of different varieties, and a DVD player reeling a string of continuous footage. In the sanctuary itself were more arrangements, pungent floral sprays and wreaths and crosses of yellow gladiolas and white carnations and daisies and tulips, and an LCD projector casting more Greta onto a white screen to the soft, elevator rhythms of Kenny G.

And there, red roses dappled the sleek black casket like cartoon paint splotched on freshly lain tar. An open viewing was macabre to Margaret, too wax museumish, and thus at her insistence it would remain closed, allowing the attendees to remember Greta as they would.

This was a reunion, of sorts, and it was difficult for some of the younger ones not to treat it as such. Sad eyes spoke, *we'll catch up later*. And those who attended only as dates felt the tone and played the part, which wasn't difficult in this place where no one smiled, and everyone cried openly and everyone hugged firmly, and everyone loved each other as if this were to be their last meeting.

Everyone, that is, except three. William Cruz III, dressed in church clothes, resembled more an Everyman Smith than the heritage his surname would suggest; and Chris and Catherine Dildy avoided all greetings and the condolence processional to preserve their own anonymity.

And, together yet apart, the three cried, prayed, apologized and left, each feeling in their own way responsible for a distance-killing of this girl they'd never known.

3. Aftermath

It had been a long afternoon, and Bob and Margaret were sapped. The car was packed full of Greta's things, and they decided there they would remain until they'd finished this chapter. A few arrangements adorned the front porch, sent FTD from those unable to travel.

The parents left those there, too, like funeral police tape, or huge talismans.

The house was sad. There were empty creaks and it did not welcome light. It seemed to have settled, to be slouching a bit. Even a first time visitor, as perhaps a tourist in a historic district, would have noticed something wrong in the den, a vacancy on the brick chimney.

Last week it was a home, even though Greta had moved away.

But now there were two.

Margaret sat on Greta's bed, fingering the lace frill on a pillowcase where there lay a single strand of hair. The closet door was open for that one last outfit. A CD case lay open by the player, which had never been turned off from her last visit. Otherwise, the room was still in boxes in the car.

Margaret *did* need now to unpack, she wavered. She was sure her baby would be visiting that night.

Bob sat in that den and stared at that chimney, the day's mail in front of him. For some reason, this evening, he methodically opened and read everything. He opened the credit card offers from Capital One and American Express, obeying the instructions on the envelope to "Do Not Discard." He opened the folded coupon packet from Harris Teeter offering specials on diapers and formula. He opened the Tide liquid detergent sample and sniffed the scent of fresh rain. He opened the propaganda from lawyers selling sue-packages.

There were Greta's spring semester grades from Brinkley and he put those aside for a stronger time.

And there, beneath it all, was the envelope from Coastal with the necessary assistance for the next phase of this tragedy. When Bob had bought the plan for his daughter, he had opted into the $350,000 coverage for bodily and property damage liabilities; and when questioned, the claims adjuster, a Jennifer-somebody, appeared comfortable that Coastal would pay, because Greta indeed was not the driver.

Dear Valued Claimant:

We regret to inform you that the recent claim filed for **Greta Ann Mackenzie 10016926** has been denied in accordance with policy **29.II.(b.): Contributory Negligence**. Please refer to your personal auto policy handbook, or contact your local agent for further clarification.

As always, it has been our pleasure to serve you.

Automotively yours,
Your Coastal Insurance Family

4. Power of the People

William Cruz III knew he was a good man. He knew this, not the way the sharp dressed man gets the second look, or the gift giver from the thank you note or tax statement, the way they know because they are acknowledged.

Monty had sound confidence and a soulful intuition.

He didn't need to be told, which made him an even better man.

He was currently single but not blissfully so. He dated around, strictly outside the Force, but he shied away from commitment, recognizing the term for what it was. Cruz told the ladies he had his selfish limitations; colloquially, he just wasn't ready to be tied down.

Today, though, he had a different take. He wanted a partner. He wanted female companionship in a fairy tale land of let's-dream-together, with whom he could horseback ride to that place far, far away where nobody knew his name. He wanted someone to hold him, someone beautiful and soft and delicately fragranced, yet someone strong enough to fend off the vipers at his doorstep.

Because this thing had already gotten way, way out of control, and it had very little if anything to do with his mode of thinking, as Cleary had warned. Cruz wasn't playing mind games of "if onlys," and hadn't lost any sleep over his ultimate decision. Alone, in perfect communion with the Lord his Savior, Monty was stable, quite fine in fact.

But alas, nothing was done in isolation. The powers of the written word, and of the people, were stronger than him. Cleary had forewarned this as well.

The Meadowmont Times had run an editorial, the opinion column, and three scathing letters to the editor against the officer. The local news stations broadcasted it on the six, the eleven, and the following day's sunrise series. This morning it was printed in the Buffalo News by The Associated Press, as his parents informed him some 800 miles away. And, just this afternoon, as he was about to bite into a German bologna and cheese sandwich on fresh pane paisano, plenty of good mustard, a call came from the producer of the nationally syndicated Perry Winters *Live!* offering to fly him cross-country for his story.

He'd been pushing pencils all week at the direction of the captain, not as punishment per se but to keep him out of the public eye. This didn't stop the picketers, who began marching this morning brandishing signs from "MPD = **M**ight **P**rotect after **D**onuts" to "Alcohol and Police do not mix." There were two pieces of anonymous hate mail waiting for him when he returned from work, and three hang ups from restricted numbers.

Monty sat on his back porch with dinner on his lap, watching mama and daddy cardinal flick and flirt around the feeder. He thought about his life, and about the seven years he'd spent in this small city. He liked it here, but that satisfaction had been cloistered in the department. He yearned for a different topic of conversation---*so, honey, how was your day?*---from a neutral party; one who was sympathetic, yet detached. Counselor Sheila in the department was not providing.

In two months he would be thirty-three. He needed a new perspective. He thought about the funeral, and thought again about what'd been. Thirty-three was not a guarantee. He recalled a proverb, probably ancient Chinese, which read, "To be uncertain is to be uncomfortable. To be certain is to be ridiculous."

This evening, Monty Cruz was very uncomfortable.

Again, if the recent and forecasted hype were to be contained in a vacuum, then Cruz's stalwart constitution would permit him to coast. But he was given the gift of intuition, and he knew a lot of people were going to bat for him, people he loved and respected, and that a few were second-guessing themselves. It was all so easily read.

He was lowering morale. He was bringing down an entire department.

Monty Cruz knew he was a good man, but he also knew he could be replaced. No one was the best. His granddaddy taught him that. Monty knew his time had come.

His time had come. He'd submit his letter to Sergeant Cleary tomorrow, first thing.

Then, he'd get on his horse, and ride.

5. Character Development

Beth said I could have her car for the day if I dropped her off at school. She'd get a ride home with Marnie, she said. Jeesh, Marnie Root was my first grade teacher, and she was old then. You gotta be old to have a name like Marnie.

So the deal was, I'd drop Beth off then go take trig, the last exam of my junior year. I'd return some movies and pay the late fee and run by the post office and get some gas---any station was fine, in Beth's car--- and I'd grab some lunch; and, if there was time, I'd return for store credit the chip crisper she'd bought at Brookstone.

And then, because Beth said I really ought to, I'd go to the funeral, on behalf of the same "best friend" who hadn't yet apologized for the hang up. I didn't share with Beth his AA appeal because I already knew what she'd say and I didn't need to hear it. These people, they just didn't seem to realize how hard this was on me, too, especially with the addition of the newest wrinkle: that Detective Scott insisted we meet tomorrow, with or without attorney Javier Rubenstein.

There definitely must be some Biblical reference to the JOB initials of my name.

If I hadn't made such a mess of sociology this would have been a banner semester because trigonometry was cake and I had an A going into it, and I was the first to congratulate myself with a pint of vodka, *no receipt, thank you*; vodka, because Slang said at his basement party that you can't smell vodka on the breath when a stoned Chat brought up the Altoids incident.

So I knocked back an eye-watering swallow of the isopropyl alcohol---and man, that *wasn't* good, but I was in it for the effect--- and I bought a cranberry cocktail chaser at the gas station---just couldn't drink it straight, like bourbon---and, mildly medicated, I mailed some letters and returned some movies; I bought a sandwich from Schlotzky's, and I even returned the crisper for $76.04 store credit

And finally, priorities out of the way and a ½ pint of vodka stronger, I drove out to Braxton in time to catch the Dildys escorting each other into the Dodd Funeral Home.

Damn, they weren't supposed to be there, because the newest plan now was to hold my own little service in the adjacent CVS parking lot with Misters Popov and Marley, to information-gather and take roll, and on the ride back to drop the grudge and call Brian, demonstrating my loyalty even though he never apologized.

But then I realized, *it's all good*. The Dildys probably don't want to be noticed anyhow. Speaking to them might just blow their cover, and so it would be extraordinarily conscientious of me *not* to speak to them. It's absolutely possible I still attended.

Jason Braswell, you truly have a gift.

"Jason, is that you?"

Oh shit, here we go. Vodka bottle tossed. Bag too. Didn't take receipt. Let's rock.

The dog crashed through the backyard screen door first, tripping up Bill at his heels, and bounded towards me, tongue hanging out. Surprised he hadn't bitten the thing off yet, big ol' dope. Dopey dog, he was.

"Hey, there, Daddy-O. What's the word?"

"Huh?"

"Nevermind." I eased the dog away from my crotch, though I was a tad amused by the thought of how good that might feel.

"Right. Okay, listen, Jason, I've got three things here I need to discuss with you. Let's-"

"-hold, hold, gotta pee first."

"Okay, well, I'll be out back. Come out when you're done."

"Rightee-O."

Despite what Slang had advised, I didn't trust the vodka. I sure felt like I smelled of alcohol. I got a beer from the fridge and took a swallow. There. Now I smelled of the beer I'd just opened. Sheer genius.

"A beer?" he asked, looking at his watch. "Oh? Okay, I guess so. Thought it was earlier than that. Be careful, now. You know my history with the stuff."

I nodded, knowing nothing about his history with the stuff.

"Anyhow, Jason, three things." He had a file folder in front of him, labeled "Jason," which he opened. "First, I got this flier from Windsor, my prep school alma mater don'cha know." I knew. "And they're advertising a full week of SAT prep courses in mid July. Now-"

"-Dad, I'm already enrolled in-"

"-listen. These begin when your Saturday classes end, these will be more intensive and *certainly* better quality." Certainly. "And besides, think of how good this will look on that Yale application."

Sigh. No point now. Not of sound mind, anyhow. "Can I think on it? Talk it over with Mom?"

"Not long. Deadline's in a week, though I could probably pull some strings, buy us some time." Sure you got the extra money? "Okay, second. I got this information from the Peace Corps"---*the Peace Corps talk again*---"wahwahwawahwah and read it over for me, okay?"

"Sure thing," I said, taking the booklet and thumbing through it, feigning interest like I'd just opened it on Christmas morning. *This is great. Thanks.* "I've got time, now that exams are over."

"Good. My experience in Nigeria was invaluable. It would make me so proud for you to have the same benefit. Now, the third thing, let's see. What was the third thing?"

I drank from my beer as he shuffled through the file. I didn't know why Beth bought Miller, for company only because she drank scotch. Horrible stuff, Miller was, unless you're already cooked. I could even taste it over the Popov.

She and I, we needed to talk.

"Okay, here it is. Probably nothing to it, but any idea how this receipt got in my car?"

CHAPTER SIX

SIX MONTHS LATER

1. William Cruz III

Six months later, Monty Cruz was unrecognizable. Bearded, tanned, and shoeless, he sold authentic Zuni turquoise jewelry and carved animal fetishes from a lotus-type position atop hand woven throws on the street market in Old Town Albuquerque, New Mexico. A tourist trap, yes, but as a tourist himself four months ago he had madly fallen for Kwanita Liseli, and now "worked" for her father.

Mr. Liseli owned an adobe bungalow which he rented to Monty, cheap. Within walking distance of the university it had previously been occupied by frat boys, who kept Mr. Liseli very busy.

But Monty, he could tell, was *skah apenimon*, "the good white man."

Saying goodbye to Meadowmont was difficult, but necessary. Sergeant Cleary accepted his resignation with courteous reluctance, and the captain himself apologized it had come to this; and the entire department saw him off with extravagant fanfare because they understood, respected, and admired his selfless decision. He was not quitting from cowardice, but resigning with honor.

His only return was when he was subpoenaed for the Dildy trial, but by then he ceased to be of interest to anyone. Like a one-hit-wonder, he had come and gone.

Monty had entertained the idea of going into education lateral entry, teaching high school English. He knew the subject matter, and he definitely had the personality for it, but after a bit of research he was appalled by the extensive state and local requirements that made it no wonder there was such a teacher shortage.

Besides, he realized he could wait tables for more money and far less hassle, he might get a meal or two out of it, and he wouldn't have to get someone to watch his customers while he ran to the bathroom.

No, he was done with all that top-down stuff for a while, the whole political morass. Monty just needed to get out, and this was the time.

Besides, he knew, because he had considered everything so carefully, that Granddaddy was smiling upon him, that he was proud of the man this boy had become.

2. Robert and Margaret Mackenzie

Six months later, the Mackenzies were still keeping separate night schedules, Robert falling asleep on the den couch to late night television, and Margaret retiring early amidst the unfinished scrapbooks and photo albums. On occasion, the two would wake up beside each other, but that was merely out of nineteen years' habit.

They weren't in strife, and they still loved each other they said, in passing and out of habit; but the loss of their daughter had extinguished all the drive and desire for each other that they were recently so demonstrative about.

They had done well by Greta. She was the result of their union.

But now she was gone, and the bedrock was crumbling.

Financially they were indeed struggling, but not despairingly so. Greta's life insurance plan covered all the hidden costs of the funeral, and medical paid a good portion but with copay and the deductible they were still tens of thousands of dollars in debt. Bob wanted to sell the house, while Margaret wanted Greta to always know where they were.

"This is the only home she's known, Bob. She won't be able to feel comfortable in any new place."

Bob let Margaret's newly-found transcendental side be.

They knew they should seek the counseling the reverend had suggested, just like they knew they still needed to update their wills, especially now, and to decide on life's next thing; for though he had retired, and she had taken "indefinite leave," they were both too young, and far too fragile, for sheer idle time.

Robert and Margaret each testified in the trial of the People versus Brian Christopher Dildy with very emotional victim impact statements that helped the jury render a very unsatisfactory verdict, though they knew from the start that their brand of justice was draconian, in this country at any rate.

They had received a few weeks ago a thick envelope from Christopher and Catherine Dildy, which they filed unopened.

The Mackenzies were not even remotely near that stage.

3. Brian Christopher Dildy

Six months later, Brian Christopher Dildy had served forty-three days of a twenty-four month sentence in the minimum security state correctional facility.

Indeed, the grand jury had returned a true bill on the voluntary manslaughter charge, and Brian was again arrested and printed and photographed but was soon after released to the care of his parents, without bond. Stan assured the magistrate that Brian was going nowhere, and he had Chris and Catherine's word on that.

Brian was as ready as he was going to get for time behind bars, as mentally prepared as one leaping into open water off the South African coast with a chain mail chum suit. He'd begun researching prison life on the internet, and almost paid $39.99 to an inmate who called himself Clean, who guaranteed the ropes for a smooth transition, but Sid in the Program changed Brian's mind.

Sid was a bank robber who had done thirteen years' hard time in a federal penitentiary. They said they could link him to twenty-two First Union heists, but Sid only recalled ten. Sid spent much of his criminal life in a haze of cocaine, but whisky was the catalyst. Take away the alcohol, and he might have had a clean slate.

Sid was a carpenter and he had his own business. He was doing very well for himself, well enough to hire Brian until it was time for him to pay his debt to society. Sid sponsored Brian through a thorough first three steps, and he kept him occupied with carpentry and conversation and homework assignments, and he eased his mind and he scared the shit out of him and he taught him how to pray.

When Jason called Brian after Greta's funeral, Brian apologized for his blow-up and he hoped they could get together again soon, maybe catch a ballgame or the new Johnny Knoxville flick, or toss the pigskin around.

'Sides, dude had to meet Sid, Brian said.

Dude suddenly had a lot of other things to do.

Brian ended the lease on his apartment and moved in permanently, so to speak, with his folks, and his original back-in-the-mind thought Was to give Roz to Jason; just give, because Roz was getting on in years and they'd shared some memories, she and Jason.

But Jason's sudden lack of interest in anything-Brian found him giving the car to Sid, who'd in turn give it to his niece who had just gotten her permit. Brian felt really good about the deal, the least he could do for this fellow AA who'd given him a job; who had listened patiently to his endless regrets and fears; and who had shared unabashedly his own experience, strength and hope.

If they thought they had a chance, the prosecution would have pursued second degree murder, but that delved into the tricky realm of malice, or intent, and there was none to be proven here. Voluntary, a class D felony, generally involved your textbook crimes of passion and was therefore a stretch, but they needed to aim high -five and a half years- and silently pull for the compromise between it and involuntary, class F.

So the prosecution did their homework, and the file was thick. Subpoenaed to the stand was Jason Braswell, to testify under oath that Brian had been drinking and driving that Friday, and to verify the time frame of his consumption that Friday; and, with the subpoenaed Charles Parker and John Hedley, to testify that Brian drank and drove regularly.

That he did, repeatedly, abuse alcohol, and that he was, in a sense, a "repeat offender."

"Objection."

"Sustained. The jury will disregard that last statement."

"Sorry, your Honor."

"Are there any more witnesses, Mr. Prosecutor?"

Yes, indeed there were. The most damning. Testimony was permitted from those most significantly affected by the crime. Robert and Margaret Mackenzie and neighbor Thomas Stiltson took the stand with heart-wrenching recollections.

Emma Jean Stiltson simply did not have the strength.

Finally, the results from the State Bureau of Investigation revealed a blood alcohol content of .31. "Not only did Brian Christopher Dildy continue drinking after he was given the blessing of a warning from Officer Cruz, but he drank nearly four times the legal limit, *and he drove, AGAIN.* Members of the jury, that is not simple carelessness. That is blatant, in your face defiance, in itself a very dangerous characteristic."

If Brian hadn't followed Stan's advice, most definitely the prosecution would have won that case. However, armed with 162 signatures for approximately 140 consecutive days of AA attendance, obviously doubling-up on a few; and a documented alcohol assessment from a certified clinician; and a full psychological evaluation, the jury unanimously agreed to two years, with parole eligibility after eighteen months.

Essentially, a class E felony. An alphabetical compromise.

On one of his first nights in prison, a night he fell asleep from the sheer exhaustion of staying awake, Brian had a dream. It was spurred by a program he'd watched on the History Channel. Lore holds that during the French Revolution, a doctor who was to be beheaded for treason told the executioner that once his head was placed in the lunette, he would begin blinking; and that, after the guillotine blade fell, he'd continue to blink until his brain shut off, indicating a horrifying brief period of consciousness following decapitation.

In the dream, Brian was the executioner, and when he picked up the head from the basket it was Greta who blinked back. Brian awoke in a scream. Someone called *here, fishy fish.* There were giggles.

And every night for the first month at lights-out he would curl up in a fetal ball beneath the burlap sheet and whimper and shake, and despite the sock he crammed in his mouth they'd hear it through his nose, and they would giggle, and fish for hours.

He'd found a very crinkled, folded piece of torn-out loose leaf on his floor. On it was a penciled, finely detailed sketch of a fish roasting over an open pit, skewered from behind by an enormous phallus.

In that hoary translucence of sleep, rubberbanded and toothpicked creatures undulated and jilted to random sounds: the minor key of the soprano soloist from a boys choir in the hollowed-out church amalgamated to kazoo-voiced ritualistic chants of torture, distant thunder over choppy black lake water, howling wind tunnels and bamboo wind chimes, the resonance from mouth-blown stoneware jugs and stovepipes, the continuous drone of Indian stringed instruments, the last sucking sounds of dishwater down the drain.

Everything about prison life he could not share with Chris and Catherine, like the hauntings, he wrote in letters to Sid, sometimes three a week. And Sid would respond, not in frequency, for he still did construction; but in length, sometimes three front and back pages of college-ruled.

And everything Brian could share with his folks, like everything else, he did. He journaled, and he even used it as a verb so he could see his mother's smile. He talked about his childhood, selecting specifics from a thick catalogue featuring *The Very Best of*.

Like the time the three of them went white water rafting and grilled the trout he and Dad had caught off the pebbly shore.

Or when he had climbed so high up the tree, and Mom scaled up to guide his feet down. He had no idea Mom could climb.

He thanked them for their parenting, for his father's openness about the disease and his mother's strength and dedication and their collaborated determination to make it work. Through his parents alone he'd been given the tools to restructure what nature presented.

He'd just laid them aside for another, more convenient time.

He apologized for their suffering, and they had no reservations about his sincerity. To the stone throwers, and there were many, it was murder by a drunk. In his parents' eyes it was a horribly tragic mistake, a very bad decision.

But for the grace of God go I. Chris Dildy, for one, had been eligible on many occasions for a similar outcome.

But Chris Dildy went to AA, where, once he got honest, he found an entirely new design for living. And as Catherine would readily attest, a miracle occurred, a complete transformation.

A total body makeover.

Forty-three days in prison, and Brian was faithfully attending the twice a week AA sessions. He knew he no longer had to, but a seed had been planted. He'd become more spiritual in his thinking and in his actions. When he wasn't writing, he read; when he wasn't reading, he prayed.

He prayed a lot for Jason Braswell, whom Brian knew was drinking very heavily. Though he'd received reports from the outside, in the latter stages of their friendship Brian saw the disintegration. At the time, he chalked it up to circumstance; but today, from his studies and his own acceptance, he cited the drug.

Brian Dildy wouldn't forgive himself for the death of Greta Ann Mackenzie for a long, long time. A letter needed to be written to Robert and Margaret, but his own parents had just sent one and he knew, anyhow, that neither would be read for a long, long time.

Regardless, Brian needed to make a personal amends before he could begin his own absolution, but apologies made too early were self-aggrandizing and trite.

He'd only served forty-three days of what he felt, planning to be on his best behavior, would be an eighteen-month sentence. He had plenty of time to apologize.

Brian was advised by Sid to count up, not down.

Counting down, he still had 506 days remaining, if he remained on his best behavior.

And, whether you're vacationing in Maui or confined to a six by eight cell, 506 days is a long, long time.

4. Jason Ottomar Braswell

It is six months later. I am halfway into my senior year and my collegiate path has been narrowed down to the state university, the state college, and the local Jesuit school known for its basketball program. In the fall, Dad and I toured the western part of the state and I had two interviews that he had arranged, his back-up plans for me should Yale not come through for him.

With *his* name and the Windsor SAT course on the application, the man truly thought I had a shot; however, with my still-abysmal SAT performance on the second go-round, and a string of extracurricular quits, and the application decomposing in some landfill, I truly knew I'd be local the next four years.

Windsor, though, was a good time. For some reason I pictured a week of New Hampshire boarding school life to be pizza and movie nights, regular black coffee, and Penthouse Forum for the truly deviant, but what I got was grass and half kegs of beer. Nightly.

And don't worry, dude. I represented the middle class well.

Mom received a Fulbright to teach English in Italy, so I am living with Dad and Beth. I could have traveled abroad with her, but I preferred instead to see out my high school career at Premier. And, to claim full responsibility for her Toyota.

Call it my graduation gift, the option *not* to go.

I passed up a trip to Italy for a ride, the freedom to stray, to do my thing at my pace on my schedule, to leave under the seat whatever the hell I wanted and to never have to call Dad for that ungodly 2:30 a.m. pickup.

Naples, on the Tyrrhenian Sea. Azure waters, fine food, gorgeous women all named Marie, for a brief opportunity to experience the majesty of an around-the-clock adult privilege.

I'm the driver now, and I drive everywhere, all the time. I drive to the airstrip and cul-de-sac construction sites to drink with people whose names have become canonized through drug culture chatter. One cat's name is Jesse Barone, a hacky sack playing, Teva wearing, throwback pothead who goes to Lincoln, the neighborhood school I'd have attended if my parents didn't think I had Braswell potential.

Also a senior, and looking to travel West to attend an institution where I interviewed, Jesse and I have much in common, and through his reputation I have met many new people and have come to feel almost popular myself.

I feel now that I've got it all.

I've got the Wyoming id, which has actually become unnecessary because my face is known. I've got the id, and I've got the popular friend who doesn't discriminate between substances and therefore allows so many new doors to open for me.

I've got that, and I've got the car as you know.

But, you know what else I have? I have an old man who doesn't want to be bothered. I mean, shit, I've reeled off so many ridiculous off-the-cuff lies about smells and whereabouts, and receipts, and either I'm really good or the guy's a complete idiot; or again, he'd just assume let it be.

No harm's been done, after all.

And then you have Brian's dad, the opposite extreme. Dude was forever tellin' Brian his story, referrin' to what he called "yets," as in, say, "I haven't gotten a DWI, *yet*." He said the word was his acronym for "you're eligible too." Jesse and Jed, and Chat, and sometimes Slang, and I, we agree Brian's day was coming because he was programmed to think that way, like he purposefully sabotaged himself because he'd been brainwashed by his father.

Whatever. The point is, I've got a sweet deal. My dad is hands-off about my drinking; figures, I guess, that I can handle the adult responsibility, or he doesn't foresee a problem to begin with.

Dude's an alcoholic. He oughta know.

Shit, maybe this is the only area where I've made him proud, this perceived responsibility, and therefore he leaves me alone about it.

Sometimes, the unfamiliar faces in the different circles I come across had already heard of me through my acquaintance with Brian Dildy, whose name has become legend through small city pop culture. I've found something sexy in this wee bit of notoriety, and I've played it out fully with the ladies who've been attracted to the bad boy mystique.

So much so, in fact, that I've cleverly eased it in to pick-up conversations. But I am careful. I don't want word getting around that I'm proud my friend is incarcerated.

Quite frankly, I'm uncertain how I feel about that whole thing. After they pulled the plug on Greta, Brian changed. Instantly. He went from a fuck-it-all, I'm-gettin'-it-all-in type, tomorrow's-no-guarantee-and-I-ain't-nappin' rapscallion to a damn, I don't know, a shaman, or something. He began to make me uncomfortable, especially when he talked about this Sid character and how they went out for coffee and to the movies together and shit. I was like, *dude, movies?*

Though Jed and I did go see *Jackass 2*, but we got baked before it so it was cool. I couldn't imagine seeing that movie straight, especially not with another dude. I wonder if they sat right next to each other, Brian and this AA Sid dude. Gives me the creeps, is what it does.

I've gotten two pretty long letters from Brian since he's been in the pen. I think it makes Dad uneasy receiving mail stamped Correctional Facility on the envelope, as if the postal worker will town-cry our consorting with criminals; that, or he worries Huey---or Dewey, or Louie, whichever Brian was--- can still negatively impact me from the inside.

I had, after all, bought him that pint because he was grieving so. Dad still brings up the receipt, from time to time, when attempting to teach a responsibility lesson, about littering, or DUI vehicular manslaughter.

The letters themselves appear to be written by a different person. I feel a sari-wearing pan flautist oughta be somewhere near, like the dude's been smokin' some whacked-out prison herb that has tinted everything technicolor, talkin' about finding "his God," and beginning his search for a "new serenity."

Right. From the way I understand it, dude's new God is a big hairy bad ass called Thing, and his only peace now would be the arrival of a fresh bitch. We talk about these letters a lot, me and Jesse, and Jed and

Chat and sometimes Slang, and we all agree that this is all a defense mechanism, like sayin' it makes it so.

Slang said prison is the absence of God on earth. That's why there are so many repeat offenders, because it is a place God has abandoned. Makes sense to me.

I did send Brian a letter about a week ago. I felt like I was signing a yearbook.

But I also likened it to visiting the elderly in assisted living:

The dude, he's probably just happy to have heard from me.